IT'S NOT LOVE, IT'S BUSINESS

ELLE WRIGHT

This is a work of fiction. Any references to historical events, real people, or real places are used fictitiously. Other names, characters, places, and events are products of the author's imagination, and any resemblance to actual events or places or persons, living or dead, is entirely coincidental.

It's Not Love, It's Business

Paperback ISBN: 978-0-9994213-9-0

Excerpt from *It's Not Me, It's You*

Elle Wrights Books, LLC

Ypsilanti, Michigan

www.ElleWright.com

Editor:

Rhonda Merwarth

Rhonda Edits

Proofreading:

Paulette Nunlee

5-Star Proofing

Cover Design:

Sherelle Green

How one night turned into fifteen and counting is beyond me. I never imagined ending up here. I'm a Marriage Broker, not a matchmaker… Especially for myself! It was always a ruse. Perception, not reality. For a purpose, not for always. Business, not romance.

Want to know my plan? A simple assist, a favor.

Want to know my potential downfall? *Him.* His sincere eyes, his intoxicating smile, his scintillating personality. Oh, and our out-of-control chemistry.

Formal galas, public dinner dates... that's what this was supposed to be. Lazy mornings, Netflix and chill, impromptu road trips… that wasn't our thing. Until it was.

Spoiler alert: I can't resist him, so I won't. Everything is bad but he's so good. Ironic, huh? I thought so too. Just like I thought this arrangement was only temporary. Except… what if it's everlasting love?

Dear Reader

Sometime ago, I embarked on this journey to write about the Young Family. While I knew this series would be a game changer for me, I didn't know how much it would challenge me.

Dallas Young had a rep to protect, not just with the public, but with herself and her family. I loved that she was unapologetic about her ambition and her candor. She was a true boss. I LOVED her.

I introduced Preston in my Once Upon a Funeral novella, Finding Cooper. I knew that he was for Dallas, but I didn't know him. Writing his story has been a highlight of my career. I so enjoyed him.

I told myself that I wouldn't go into this series unwilling to let my characters do the talking. So far, every single Young sibling has transformed these books into something amazing. These characters tell their stories to me in ways that frustrate me, but I'm so glad that I let them lead.

It's Not Love, It's Business is a story is dear to my heart, and the perfect book commemorate my 25th release! I hope you enjoy their journey.

Love,
Elle
www.ellewright.com

P.S. Don't kill me for the plot twist!

Recommended Reading

MEET THE YOUNG FAMILY

It's Not Love, It's Business is not the first book featuring a member of the Young Clan. If you'd like to get acquainted with this family before you read, I recommend starting with the following books:

IT'S NOT ME, IT'S YOU is book one in the Young In Love Series. I would highly suggest you start with that story.

The Young Family have also appeared in several of my other novels/novellas.

Paityn Young found everlasting love in my Park Manor novella, HER LITTLE SECRET. The twins, Blake and Bliss made their first appearance in her story.

Blake Young appeared again as Ryleigh's friend in my Once Upon a Baby novella, BEYOND EVER AFTER.

Duke Young burst onto the scene in my Pure Talent novels, THE WAY YOU TEMPT ME and THE WAY YOU HOLD ME. And he stole the show.

Dallas Young made her presence known in my Once Upon a Funeral novella, FINDING COOPER.

Please Note: Several of these stories take place around the same time. Some events may happen in multiple books from a different POV.

www.ellewright.com

For Lina, thanks for being you. You are an inspiration to me.

Dick Hangover

A DALLAS YOUNG ORIGINAL

Dallas

October, Last Year

Crazed…or crazy? It could've been either or both. *Crazed*, because this man was too fly, too fine, too sexy, too off-limits to resist. *Crazy*, because the invisible line that had kept me in check during our years-long, sorta-friendship was pretty much non-existent. In about three minutes, I was going to do something I probably—no, definitely—shouldn't do. Like fuck Preston Hayes.

It was his damn fault. He'd entered the venue earlier, dressed in the perfect costume. His World War II Soldier to my muthafuckin' Carmen Jones. My sister Bliss might've called it destiny, but nah… I wouldn't go that far. Happenstance was the better word. Could I really waste the chance to fulfill a fantasy? *Still…*

I tried to never make the same mistake twice, no matter how horny I was. Hooking up with a friend of a friend was a no-no. I'd learned that hard lesson a long time ago. And fucking a sorta-but-good friend was a disaster waiting to happen. Especially since I had no intention of ever doing him again. *Yet…*

Despite him looking all kinds of hot in that uniform, the night had started innocently enough. We'd exchanged quick side hugs and toasted my birthday. Sometime between nine o'clock and Juvenile's voice ringing "Cash Money Records taking over," things had taken a turn. I'd noticed him dancing with some woman. And I hated it. Hated *her*. For just a brief second before I'd snapped myself out of that shit. I hadn't been quick enough, though. Because he'd recognized my slip. Then, I'd seen the mischievous—and entirely too damn sexy—smirk spread across his full lips. *But…*

The mood had been set from the moment our eyes had met across the dance floor. It was his lips for me. And his body. And his eyes. Shit, it was just him. He was serious, but never took himself too seriously. Funny, but not clown-like. Smart as hell, but he didn't know it all. Sexy, but subtle about his shit. *And…*

He'd joined me shortly after his dance, overwhelming me with his tall frame, his baritone voice, his cologne. The music, the drinks, and the conversation amped up the sexual tension. Yet, there were no shots fired, no flirtatious brushes of my hand against any part of his body. There *was* witty banter, frank language, and mutual respect—the way we'd always been with each other. Except… I knew tonight was his night. *Our night.*

As he led me across the dance floor, away from prying eyes and nosy siblings, I experienced an uncommon emotion for me. Anticipation. Odd development, considering I wasn't an overly emotional person, which benefitted me personally and professionally. And unlike my sister, I hadn't put myself on punishment from yak or dick, so I wasn't willing to hump any dick that presented itself to me. I loved sex. Hell, my last good orgasm had been just over two weeks ago. But it'd been a while since I'd craved it *this* badly. I wanted what I wanted. *Him*. For one night only.

The click of the lock interrupted my thoughts; the echo of his footsteps against the bathroom tile brought me back to reality. A rush of adrenaline shot through me as he approached me. Just outside the door, my party was in full swing, my sisters were probably looking for me, my parents were more than likely doling out relationship advice to our friends, and the DJ would cue the birthday song in a matter of minutes.

"How do you want it?" His voice was a low, smooth confirmation of what was to come. Leaning closer, he murmured against my ear, "Because I'm ready to give it to you."

Oh, the possibilities. Hard and fast was my only requirement. Hard, because I liked it that way, and fast, because it was almost time for cake.

"Surprise me," I murmured. Usually, this was the point of the evening when I'd take control, get my orgasm and bounce. But my feet were rooted to the floor as I waited for him to make the first move.

His gaze dropped to my mouth, and I braced myself for a kiss, the brush of his lips against mine. If I was going to break my own personal rule and have sex with Preston, I wanted all of him. I wanted his arms around me, his tongue on my skin, and his dick in my pussy. Full stop. Given my desire for him in that moment, I could've been swayed to let him cuddle me a quick second before I made my exit. *Maybe.*

Seconds passed, and the kiss never came. *Dammit,* I wanted it. Instead, he treated me to his slow smile, the intoxicating hint of mint and tequila on his breath, his hooded gaze on mine, his hands gliding over my hips to my ass. *Shit.* Maybe I didn't need the kiss. His tongue darted out and licked his lips. *Oh, my.* I definitely needed it.

Stepping up on the tips of my toes, I kissed him, sucking his bottom lip into my mouth and biting down on it hard. The groan that escaped his mouth shot straight to my core.

Hot, bothered, and extremely wet, I was prepared to hop up on the counter and get the show on the road. Before I could move, though, he spun me around and smacked my ass. "Bend over. I want you like this."

I peered at his reflection in the mirror. His intense stare nearly took my breath away. Four words flitted through my mind on repeat. *One night. One fuck.*

He unzipped my red skirt, and it fell to the floor. "Bend over," he commanded softly.

Leaning forward, I arched a challenging brow. "Alright now, Hayes. But just so you know…once we leave this bathroom, we're right back to me not giving a fuck about your orders."

He smirked. "But until then…"

Oh, damn. Preston was too damn sexy for my own good. Maybe tomorrow I'd sit down and try to figure out why. For now, I'd settle for the heat of the moment or the shots or the costumes—whatever it took to get to my happy place.

He traced the line of my spine with his thumb and hooked his fingers under the band of my panties. "I'll take these." The thin fabric of my thong gave way to his pull as he ripped it off and tucked the lacy material into his shirt pocket.

Finally, I did what I was told and bent over, maintaining eye contact with him. That didn't last long, though, because—*Oh, God.* My eyes fluttered closed as he brushed my clit with his talented fingers.

"No, Dallas," he prodded, slipping a finger inside me. He placed wet kisses down the back of my neck, over to my bare shoulder. "You're going to watch me fuck you." He gripped my chin with his free hand and kissed the shit out of me.

Even with his lips on mine, his tongue moving against mine, I wanted more. I moaned when he slipped another finger inside me and increased the pressure of his movements. "Hayes?" I whispered between kisses.

He didn't answer and he didn't stop. Not even when I climaxed for the first time. Not until I was on the brink of another delicious orgasm. Then, he stepped away, taking his warmth with him.

I stopped short of begging him to finish, but I wanted to simultaneously plead with him to keep going and cuss his ass out for leaving me hanging. My body felt like a live wire. Every nerve had sparked to life from his touch. I was drunk on him, helpless to resist his pull.

"Damn you," I grumbled.

He snickered. "Don't rush me." He stepped into me, letting me feel his erection against my butt. "You'll come again. Very soon."

My control snapped under the weight of his stare, the chemistry of our bodies. Thoughts of him, of us together, pushed every bit of my common sense aside. In a matter of minutes, he'd stolen my mind and my body. "Condom," I managed to get out. He'd stolen all the other words.

The only thing left to do now was wait. The moment I felt him pulsing against me, I wanted to turn around and take a look. Because the dick felt pretty damn impressive—and rock hard. But I couldn't. I wouldn't break the eye contact. A moment later, he was inside me, every thrust stealing something from me I knew I couldn't get back. He filled me completely, drove me insane with need. We came at the same time, our lips fused together, and his arms wrapped around me tightly. It was our first time—our *only* time. But it felt like we'd already mastered each other, like we'd been doing this for years.

Hung over from the experience, I knew I could fall to the floor at any moment. I sagged against the countertop, holding myself semi-upright. No sense in losing my last cool point for the night. Let's see…in the past twenty minutes, I'd offered my wordless consent for sex in the public women's bathroom of the venue where everyone was celebrating my birthday. And I wanted to beg him to do it again and again.

Dallas, get your shit together right the fuck now.

Preston buried his face in my hair, gave me a gentle kiss, and backed away, pulling up his pants before I could get a good look at the dick that had almost made me forget my common sense. He disappeared into one of the stalls.

Sighing, I glanced at myself in the mirror. Not only did I feel dick-wasted, I looked it. My pin curls were on their last leg, my black, off-the-shoulder blouse was twisted around my waist, and my cheeks were flushed.

I opened my purse and pulled out my *I-might-get-some-be-ready* kit. Inside the small bag, I had an extra set of black lace panties, the same style he'd ripped off moments earlier. I grabbed my makeup bag, a washcloth, and body wash.

Preston reappeared and watched as I cleaned myself up and touched up my makeup. He didn't speak, he just looked, his dark brown eyes seeing everything he shouldn't.

I put my lipstick on, tossed everything back into my purse, and turned to face him. "Okay, I'll talk to you later." My voice cracked, which was out of character—like everything else that had just happened between us. "We don't have to bring this up again. In fact, let's just pretend it didn't happen." Yet, even as I said the words, I instinctively knew I'd never be able to forget his scent, his taste, the sound of us together, the feel of him inside me. Still, I was definitely going to give it my best try.

He nodded. "Sounds like a plan."

I sucked in a deep breath and walked toward the door. Before I unlocked it, I said, "Thanks. Happy birthday to me." I straightened my shirt and exited the bathroom of iniquity.

Outside the bathroom, the dance floor was packed, and our closest friends were dressed up like we'd requested. Having a Halloween birthday was always a kick for me. Every year, me and my twin brothers would throw a party with a kick-ass theme. This year, it'd been my turn to pick, and I'd decided on Black Movie Characters. Lined up against the wall, several girls wore cheerleading costumes, representing Gabriel Union and her friends in *Bring It On*. My mother looked like *Foxy Brown*, and my father cracked me up as Nick Fury from *The Avengers*.

To my right, I spotted Cooper chatting with some random female. He was dressed like *Django Unchained*. For a second, I considered interrupting him but decided against it. My best guy friend was very perceptive, and he might've put two and two together. Since Preston was his best friend and business partner, it was best Coop didn't know that we'd gotten busy moments ago.

As if he sensed my presence, Coop glanced over at me. "You good?" he shouted over the music.

I nodded. "Yep." It wasn't quite a lie. I was good. My body was buzzing, on fire. But no matter what I'd said to Preston in the bathroom, I couldn't stop thinking about him. *I need a drink.*

Swallowing hard, I made a beeline toward the VIP area. On the way there, I waved at several guests but didn't talk to anyone else. My siblings were lining up shots of tequila when I stepped into the roped-off section of the venue. Tonight, only five of us were in attendance. Growing up with four brothers and three sisters was a trip, but I wouldn't trade it for anything in the world. I loved them all dearly. And I knew one or all of them would figure out where I'd been for the last several minutes. *So…*

I avoided eye contact with my sister, Blake, and turned my back on her very-pregnant twin, Bliss. I knew if I looked at either of them, they'd know my dirty little secret. Instead, I turned to the two people I'd shared my mother's womb with and grinned. Then, I took Duke's shot glass from his hand and downed the contents. Next, I snatched Dexter's glass and took his shot. And since I was on a roll, I picked up a full glass from the table and drank that one too.

Dex frowned. "What the…?"

I pointed at my brother, who looked like Ice Cube in *Boyz n The Hood*, complete with Dickies, house shoes, and a Jheri curl wig. "Shut up. No questions."

"Damn, Dallas." Duke had done the bare minimum with his costume, choosing to come as Mike Lowrey from

Bad Boys. "Where the hell you been? We've been looking for your sneaky ass for an hour." He was six minutes older than me and never could resist bossing me around in the name of being my "older" brother.

"Nunya," I told him. Because even though I was the youngest of the triplets, *I* was the boss. "Mind yours. And I wasn't gone an hour."

He waved a dismissive hand my way. "Man, take yo ass over there and sit down. That's why one of your lashes is falling off."

I gasped, struggling to open my purse and grab my mirror.

Bliss stepped over to me and took my purse from me, while Blake swooped in and ordered me to close my eyes.

"You know I can spot a freshly fucked look from a mile away," Blake muttered. My sissy was a stone-cold fox as Valkyrie from *Thor: Ragnarok*. "I never thought I'd see it on you, though."

"I thought I'd fixed it," I whisper-yelled. "This is why I don't wear these things. I should've never let Bliss talk me into all this makeup."

It only took a minute for my Super Sister to fix my lash, but it felt like an eternity. "Do better," she chided. "You know better. If you're gonna get busy, fix your face afterward."

Bliss returned with a full glass of water, her nun outfit concealing her very pregnant belly. "Sissy, you need this."

I gulped the water and plopped down on one of the sofas. "Thanks," I breathed, letting out a heavy sigh. Bliss handed me another full glass.

Duke sat next to me. "Who you been fucking?"

I choked on my water, and he patted my back. Hard. "Nobody," I lied. "Get out of here."

"I want to know too." Blake took a seat on an ottoman across from me. "Spill."

"Nobody," I repeated. "I just had a rough bathroom break."

"You're so full of shit." Blake laughed. "You've definitely been fucking someone."

"Since you won't get out of here, I'll leave." I stood up and walked to another sofa, away from them. Closing my eyes, I tried to clear my mind. *One night. One fuck.*

"Dallas?"

I yelped, jumping up. "Shit, you scared me."

Preston leaned in, and I fell back on the sofa. He sat next to me. "Listen, I—"

Hands up, I scooted away from him. "Nah, nigga, we're not doing this. We agreed on it. Go sit somewhere else."

"Does this mean I can never sit next to you again?"

"Yes," I hissed. "No. It's not that. You just can't sit next to me tonight. Distance." I waved at him. "Bye."

Preston laughed—probably at my expense. "I thought you'd want your earring back." He held up a single gold-hoop earring.

"Thanks," I grumbled, snatching it away from him. "Sorry." Before I could stop myself, my gaze dropped to his mouth. *Shit, I want to kiss him.*

The wicked smile that formed on his full lips told me he knew exactly what I was thinking. Raising a challenging brow, he said, "You sure?"

For a second, I wondered if I'd said what I'd been thinking out loud. "Huh?"

"Are you sorry?"

I blinked. "What?"

"You said you were sorry?"

"I am, about the…um…" I scratched my temple and

tried to remember why I was sorry. "I shouldn't have talked to you like that. You just caught me off guard." *In more ways than one.*

He nodded. "Ah. No problem."

"Okay." I stood, smoothing a hand over my skirt. "I should go." I hurried back to the other side of the space, grumbling a string of curses along the way.

Duke pulled me to the side and whispered in my ear, "Preston? Really, Dallas?"

Frowning, I smacked him on his shoulder. I should've known Duke would figure it out before anyone else. He was good like that. "Move, fool."

As if on cue, Blake joined us. "Sissy? Preston? What the hell were you thinking?"

I opened my mouth to speak, but I had nothing. Instead, I shrugged. "Blame it on the costume—and the tequila."

"If you're going to ruin friendships and shit, was it at least good?" Blake asked.

I bit down on my bottom lip and nodded. "Too good. *So* damn good. Like, 'if there's a cure, I don't want it' good."

Duke raised his hands in surrender. "Shit, I'm out. This is too much, even for me."

Once he was out of earshot, Blake gave me a high-five. "That's what I'm talking about."

I breathed a heavy sigh of relief. It felt good to just say it out loud. Maybe then I could forget about it? I tugged my sister over to a quiet corner. "I mean, I've had good dick before, but his deserves an award, some accolades… something to distinguish it from the rest."

Blake winked. "Ayyee." She did a little hip roll. "I'm down for the Dick Awards."

We broke out in a fit of giggles. I almost told her more,

but then there was cake and candles and my parents singing the birthday song with wide grins on their faces. As my friends and family closed in around me, Dex, and Duke, I found myself searching for the man who'd fucked me into my thirty-fourth year of life. I wondered if I'd ever be able to forget—or if I even wanted to.

Chapter One

MY LIFE

Dallas

June, This Year

"Calm down, Demi." I stepped onto the curb and glanced at my immediate surroundings. Downtown Ann Arbor was buzzing with activity, people everywhere. Couples walking hand-in-hand, dogs pulling their owners, men leering, weirdos being weird. A typical evening in my hometown. "Give me a sec." I put my AirPods in and dropped my phone into my bag. "Okay, I'm here. What's going on?"

"I'm done. Finished."

I rolled my eyes. My bestie, Demi, called at least once a week to tell me she was finished with something. It was either her man or her career. She'd recently moved to Los

Angeles and had immediately picked up a very wealthy, high-profile client—actress Paige Mills. "Is it work?" I asked, checking my watch.

"No," my friend said.

"So, it's Dorian?"

"Yes."

I sighed. "What the hell did he do this time?"

"He told me I needed to lose some weight."

"So, fuck him." At this point, we'd been friends for far too long for me to mince words. "Tell his ass to grow a dick. Since you've been complaining he can't get the job done."

"Dallas!"

I shrugged. "What?"

"Where are you?"

"I'm walking to the restaurant." I hurried across the street, nearly running into a young man in super tight shorts and light blue hair. "I told you I'm meeting Maya for dinner."

"Exactly. Which means you're out in public, loud as hell, talking about my boyfriend's dick?"

"You know I don't spend my time worrying about what people think of me. I don't live in that part of my feelings. And you shouldn't either."

Demi snorted. "I'm hanging up."

"If you hang up on me, I'm telling Blake to call you." My friend's heavy sigh let me know that was the last thing she wanted. My sister was ruthless when it came to this type of shit. After all, Blake was known as The Breakup Expert. She'd been helping women break up with their trifling men for years. "Listen, I love you. But I hate Dorian."

"I kind of hate him too," she admitted.

"Okay, then. Do something about it."

"Fine."

I stopped in front of the restaurant and peered through the window. Maya was already seated at a booth. "Shit, she's here."

"She's early," Demi said.

About fifteen minutes early, which wasn't ideal. I made it a point to be early to every occasion, whether it was dinner with my father, a pedicure with my sisters, or a work meeting. It was a personal goal to be anywhere before everyone else so I could think, formulate a plan of action. "I have to go. By the time I call you tonight, I hope you'll be single. Bye, girl." I pulled my earbuds out and set them in the case. When I reached out to open the door, a very masculine hand stopped me. I whirled on him, ready to clock whoever it was for having the audacity to touch me. "What…? You." I yanked my arm free. "This isn't happening."

"Dallas!" My ex, Kimball Payne, blocked my entrance into the restaurant. "I'm sayin'. Give me a chance."

Stepping out of arms reach, I folded my arms over my chest. "I thought I made myself very clear the last time you came to see me."

The six long months I'd spent with him were some of the worst of my life. If Kimball wasn't calling me every ten minutes for no reason at all, he was leaving mushy voicemails and texting heart emojis. I'd known from the beginning that it wouldn't last, and I'd stayed for the weekend sex. Until I couldn't even do that anymore.

"Please?" He reached for me, but I pivoted away. "Stop playin', baby. Can I just talk to you?"

He's such a punk. There was nothing worse than a beggin' man. Over the last few months, Kimball had been showing up at random places—at the neighborhood bar me and my siblings liked to gather, at my brother's gym, at my office building. And each time I'd seen him, I'd told him to fuck off. "Kim, you know I don't play games—and I don't fuck married men."

"I can explain."

"No need." When he tried to grab my hand, I balled up a fist. "If you touch me, I *will* fight you on this street. And I know you don't want that."

Kimball scanned the area, dropping his head. He played professional football for Detroit and had recently married a popular reality television star. Standing at six foot three, he was hard to miss. All it would take was one camera phone, and he'd be on the blogs. Correction, *we'd* be on the blogs. I wanted no part of that mess. "We need to talk," he murmured.

"Not really. Go home to your wife."

"You pissed me off. I was upset, so I—"

"Got married?" I shrugged.

"I thought we were done."

I nodded. "You were correct."

"I'm sorry if I hurt you."

"Get a grip, muthafucka. You didn't hurt my feelings. *I* broke up with you. Usually when that happens, people move the fuck on."

Kimball grabbed my hand. "Have dinner with me. I miss you. Don't you miss me?"

"No," I admitted. "I don't. Look, I have to go. Be happy."

I brushed past him and entered the restaurant. Glancing back over my shoulder, I saw him standing there watching me, a pitiful look on his face. I waved him on and headed toward the booth where Maya was seated.

"I'm so sorry." I bent down and gave her a hug. "I'm usually a lot earlier."

"No apology necessary," My mentor assessed me. "Besides, I see you handled yourself very well out there."

I sighed, sliding into my seat across from her. "You caught that, huh?"

"I'm always amazed at your ability to never show your ass in public, but I'm not sure I would've had your patience out there. It's time for Mr. Payne to move on."

Laughing, I took a sip of water from a full glass on the table. "I couldn't agree more."

"Besides, his wife is a trip. I watch the show every Sunday night, and she is messy."

"Tell me about it," I grumbled.

"Enough about him, though. How are you, sweetie? You look beautiful as always."

"Thank you. I feel the same about you." That wasn't a lie. "I was so happy to get your call. It's been too long."

Maya Winters was one of the best attorneys in the state. She was also a close friend of the family and my favorite professor. Going to her class had been one of the highlights of my time at Michigan Law. Even after I'd graduated and passed the bar, she'd made herself available to me, offering invaluable advice for my career and my life.

For the next few minutes, we caught up, talking about everything from basketball to the latest courthouse drama. Always blunt; I appreciated her candor. She was tough as nails in the courtroom, well-respected by everyone, and admired by many. I'd wanted to be just like her when I was younger.

"I must admit, I have ulterior motives," she admitted. "I wanted to speak with you about something important."

"Is everything okay? Is it Julia?" Maya had divorced her husband of twenty-five years and had married the love of her life, Julia. The couple had weathered the odds against them and were extremely happy. "Mom told me the treatments are going well."

Maya smiled sadly. "She's fighting a hard battle, but the doctors are optimistic. All I know is I love her, and I want her to be comfortable. And I do everything in my power to make it so."

"Please let me know if I can help in anyway."

"Actually, there is something you can do for me," she said.

"Anything."

She grinned slyly. "Are you sure about that? Because it's a big ask."

A knot formed in my stomach. "Why do I feel like I need a glass of wine for this conversation?"

"You might," she confessed, waving the waitress over and ordering a round of drinks. "As you know, I belong to several organizations."

I nodded. "Of course."

"Most of them don't matter, but one of them does. Color of Law is looking for someone, a young woman we can groom."

Color of Law was a group of amazing African American women who worked behind the scenes to encourage and increase the number of black women in the field. Its membership consisted of some of the nation's top legal minds, scholars, judges, and politicians. The moment I'd passed the bar, I'd signed on as an associate member and had attended several annual conferences over the years. But I'd been so focused on my own career, my own business, that I hadn't been able to do as much as I'd hoped.

"I immediately thought of you," she continued. "I want you to take a leadership role in the organization, learn the ropes, and eventually run for office."

My mouth fell open. Shocked wasn't even the right word. Floored was more like it. "What?"

"As you know, the political climate is horrendous. In order to make effective change, we need more black women on the bench or in positions of power in the community."

"I..." I blew out a harsh breath. "This is not what I expected."

"Of course not, dear. But I think you have what it takes."

Honestly, running for office was always a far-off kind of thing. I figured it'd be something I'd check off on my list after I turned fifty or something. But now that she'd essentially planted the seed, I couldn't help but wonder if I could make this work sooner than later.

Maya squeezed my hand. "You don't have to make a decision now. But I would like you to come and meet the board of our Michigan chapter."

"Sounds fair," I said. "Can I ask you a question?"

"Certainly."

"Why me?"

She smiled. "You're intelligent, capable, strong. You have a brilliant mind. You avoid scandal. And you're not about that bullshit. You remind me of myself at your age. Good reputation, fearless, determined, willing to do whatever it takes to get to where you want to be."

On any other day, I would've agreed with her. I was all of those things. To hear my mentor confirm it... I swallowed past a hard lump in my throat. Crying was not an option, but I damn sure wanted to. Because I'd worked my ass off to set myself apart from everyone else.

When Demi and I entered the field, we'd wanted to become giants. She helped women regain their dignity in the courtroom, and I negotiated mutually beneficial mergers between people who needed to marry for whatever reason. My siblings called me The Marriage Broker.

"That means a lot to me, especially coming from you," I told Maya. "Thank you."

"It's the truth. You know I wouldn't lie."

I chuckled. "I know."

"Dallas, I wouldn't ask if I didn't think you could do this."

"It's a lot of pressure," I admitted. "Definitely something I have to think about."

"I would expect nothing less."

We spent the next hour eating, drinking, and enjoying each other's company. By the end of our meal, I felt better about everything. As we walked to our cars, I thought about her confidence in me. "Thanks for dinner. And thanks for believing in me."

She turned to me, squeezing my arms the way she'd always done. "Always. I'll be in touch about meeting the board. I've assured them you're it, but they want to get to know you for themselves."

I nodded. "Just let me know when. I'll be there."

When we made it to her car, she opened the door and waved. "Talk to you soon."

"Definitely."

I watched her drive off and fired off a text to my sisters: *We need to talk.*

The drive to my house was uneventful, which was good, because all I could think about was Color of Law and their plans for me. I'd already debated it in my head and had analyzed the pros and cons. I'd talked to my sisters briefly and even prayed for an answer, a clue, some sort of sign. And I'd probably debate, analyze and overthink it tomorrow—and the next day. The only thing that seemed to be clear was...*I want it.*

I parked in my garage and hopped out of the car. Once inside my house, I headed to the fridge and pulled out a bottle of water. A moment later, my phone buzzed. I eyed the display and answered. "What are you doing?"

"Girl, working," Demi said. "I've been preparing this complaint for hours. Have to get it just right."

I stretched my legs and arms and leaned against the counter. "Wait 'til I tell you about dinner."

"You know I want to know. I miss Maya. Wish I could've been there."

"I needed you there. Before I start, though…did you do what you said you would do?"

"He's not here right now. But his shit is outside. That's a start, right?"

I shrugged. "As long as he doesn't bring that suitcase back in the house with his patented sob story about his childhood." I peeled a banana. "I have so much shit to do. I'm supposed to help Blake with her housewarming party this weekend, and I still haven't been to the grocery store. I'm in charge of drinks."

"Uh-oh," she grumbled.

Frowning, I bit into my banana. "What's wrong? Is he home?"

"No, but you have bigger things to worry about than drinks. Get your laptop."

Dread filled my gut. "Why?"

"Just do it."

I set the banana down and walked over to my desk. I wiggled the mouse and it powered up. Then, I entered the password and sat down. "What am I looking for?"

"Kimball Payne."

Oh, no. I tapped the keyboard with my thumb. "Before I do this… Is he dead?"

"No. But you might kill him when you see what happened."

I typed in his name and my heart sunk. "Fuck."

"You have to call Skye, because you're going to need a PR person. Now."

My best friend wasn't wrong. She was one hundred percent right. Kimball wasn't the only name trending. Mine was too. I scrolled through pages of commentary about me and the status of my relationship with my ex. Pictures of us together littered the internet, memes created of the scene outside of the restaurant earlier. Instead of attorney Dallas Young, I was now Kimball Payne's side chick and the homewrecker trying to ruin his marriage. *Shit.*

THREE MILES in sweltering hot temperatures was the perfect way to start my day, but it did nothing to ease my mind. The last couple of days had been a nightmare filled with retweets about my relationship with Kimball, nasty emails from fans of his wife, interview requests from reporters, YouTube vloggers spouting unsubstantiated rumors, and calls from concerned family and friends. Dex had nearly kicked a photographer's ass yesterday because he'd harassed me all the way into the office. Even my father had had to tell some dude off for camping out near the gate of my parents' home.

I wasn't one to let anyone see me sweat, but I'd had my share of meltdowns in the privacy of my home since the *news* had broken. Nothing was how it should've been. I should've been on cloud nine, preparing to charm the board of Color of Law and negotiating cases for my clients. But I'd been inundated with mess.

After my run, I pulled up the weeds in my yard, mowed the lawn, and turned on the sprinklers. On my way into the house, I noticed a small envelope on the porch. Picking it up, I checked for a return address on the front and back. *Nothing.*

I walked into the house, dropped my towel on the floor near the door, and opened the envelope. Fury laced through my veins as I read the fancy script:

YOU ARE CORDIALLY INVITED TO THE WEDDING OF

DALLAS YOUNG

AND

HER HO-ISH WAYS.

I HOPE YOU'RE HAPPY! LEAVE MARRIED MEN ALONE.

Hours later, I was still angry. So pissed that I didn't bother to comb my hair or make sure my clothes matched. I just showered, then hopped in my car and drove to my sister's house.

By the time I arrived at Blake's new home, I was shaking with rage. Without knocking, I barged into the house, ignoring the stunned looks of my siblings.

"What the hell is wrong with you?" Dex asked, concern in his brown eyes.

"Good question," my little brother, Asa, murmured.

I must've looked crazier than I thought, because Blake asked, "Dallas, what's up with your outfit? And that hair? Girl, why are you looking like this?"

Letting out a frustrated sigh and a terse curse, I stalked over to Blake and smacked that stupid, fucking pseudo-invitation onto the counter. "Here."

She picked up the piece of paper and read it. Her eyes widened. "I'm so confused."

"I'm getting married." I closed my palm over her

mouth. “No questions. I don’t want to talk about it.” I scanned the worried faces of my family and fought back tears. “I mean it,” I croaked. “Not a word.”

A knock on the door drew my attention there just as my parents entered the house. And I knew I had to get out of there before the dam broke and I turned into a blubbering fool. I heard Blake call my name, but I didn’t have it in me to answer any questions. So I told her I needed her to get me together, and I headed straight for her bedroom.

“Sissy?”

I glanced at Blake, who’d been working in silence, fixing my hair and putting light makeup on my face. She’d given me an outfit. Well, it was really *my* outfit that she’d borrowed months ago, but still… And she’d waited for me to talk.

She hugged me. “It’s going to be okay.”

I snorted. “You’re so sappy now.”

I’m not,” she argued. “I love you.”

“Oh God, stop.” Blake had met Professor Lennox Cole right around the time Bliss had given birth to my niece. Then, she’d fallen in love with him and had bought a freakin’ house. We were the most alike, even though she and Bliss were twins. While I was extremely close to all of my sisters, I spent the most time with Blake. “First, you turned all soft on me. Now, you’re hugging me and telling me you love me.”

She shrugged. “It’s true.”

My eyes burned with unshed tears. “I’m just angry. I’ve spent my whole life flying under the radar, laser-focused on my career. And this fool ruined everything with one unwelcome visit. I want to fuck him up.”

“Dallas, you can’t see this now because you’re so angry. But you’re not ruined. It’s one setback. You’ll fix it like you fix everything else, because that's what you do. You're the fixer."

I rested my head on her shoulder. "And you're the fighter."

"Damn right. Say the word, and I'll kick Kimball's big ass, weak ass, no-touchdown-getting ass, heart-emoji-sending ass up and down Woodward Avenue."

I laughed. "I can't with you."

"I'm so serious. And that invitation? Let me find out who sent it." She smacked her right fist against her left palm. "They can get beat down too. On sight. Nobody calls my sissy a ho."

"You called me a ho before."

"That's because you broke the leg off my brand-new Barbie doll. I loved that thing." Blake had been begging for that doll for months. It'd been an accident, but she'd hated me for a few days after that.

"How many times do I have to apologize for that?" I asked.

"Until you mean that shit."

"I'm sorry."

She bumped my shoulder. "It's okay. You've paid me back in lots of clothes since then."

"And shoes." I let out a huge sigh. "I have to get myself together."

Blake stood. "I'll leave you to it. But when you come out this room, you'd better be ready to party. We'll tackle Kimball and the hot mess he created later."

After she left, I sat with my thoughts for a moment. The anger subsided a little and I jotted down a list of things to do first thing on Monday, starting with a plan of action and ending with a conversation with Maya. It was time to take control and fix my life.

Chapter Two

ALL FALLS DOWN

Preston

Ending the day with full lips wrapped around my dick was just what the doctor ordered. The only problem was I couldn't concentrate on my nut, because my phone wouldn't stop ringing. I set my phone down next to me, rested the back of my head on the couch, and tried to get my head back in the game.

"Baby, are you okay?"

Baby? I glanced down at the beautiful woman, perched on her knees in front of me. Tabatha was her name. I couldn't remember her last name, though. Byrd…no, Burks. I ran my fingers through her hair. "I'm fine. Just work."

The call from my construction manager earlier in the day had set me off. Instead of finishing up an important project, we'd had to extend our timeline several months because of material shortages and flooding due to a week of severe weather. As if the day couldn't get any worse, one of our clients lost their funding on a future project, and the City of Detroit hadn't approved the contract for the new affordable condominium community. Since then, things had steadily declined and would probably be worse tomorrow.

"Well—" she leaned up and kissed me softly, "—maybe I can help? I'm a good listener."

She was sweet. Really. We'd met a week ago at the casino. After we'd played Blackjack, I'd taken her fine ass to the hotel. So, when she'd called and asked me to meet her at Greektown tonight, I'd assumed it'd be more of the same. Not sure how we'd graduated to terms of endearment. And talking about my life, my business? *Not gonna happen.*

"Preston?" she called, pulling me out of my thoughts. "Want to talk about it?"

Tabatha had said the magic word again. *Talk.* Still bothered by how comfortable she was and how *uncomfortable* I felt, I stared at her. For the first time since I'd arrived at her place, I wondered why I was there. She wasn't my first random hookup, but real talk…I'd grown tired of the same ol' shit. Different woman, different day. Fuck now, question everything later. I'd done my fair share of that in my twenties and now that I was pushing on forty's door, that behavior wasn't as satisfying as it once was. My life was about business, building my empire, making moves. Not this.

"Or I could always keep your mind off work?" she suggested with a wink, squeezing my dick.

My phone buzzed, breaking through the do-not-disturb setting, which more than likely meant something was wrong. Before I could pick it up, the phone vibrated again.

Shit. I snatched the device and fired off a quick *Give me a minute* text.

"Are you okay?" she asked again.

I flashed a quick smile before I stood, pulled my boxers and my jeans up, and picked up my phone. "Not really." I scowled at the message I'd received. "I should probably get outta here, though."

The soft, concerned look in her eyes transformed to an annoyed and angry glare. "Hell nah," she shouted, standing to her feet and kicking a throw pillow. "What you not gon' do is come in my house, let me suck your dick, and—"

"You didn't suck my dick," I clarified.

She rolled her eyes and flipped me off. "Whatever, muthafucka. You're not going to bounce on me like this. I don't know who the fuck you think I am."

I stepped back, surprised by the outburst. Up until now, Tabatha had portrayed herself as a mild-mannered good girl. Granted, I hadn't known her long, but she'd made it a point to tell me that first night that she didn't "do this often," which had given me pause because it'd seemed a little disingenuous. Especially since *she* was the one who'd asked to come back to *my* place. She'd also mentioned she didn't cuss because of her dead grandmother. And, supposedly, she abhorred violence. In less than a minute, she'd proven she was full of shit. Which made my decision to walk out the best one and reaffirmed I should always follow my instincts.

Tabatha snapped her fingers in my face. "Hey, you. Did you hear what I said?"

I let out a slow, deep breath and walked to the door. She followed me, calling me every type of punk, asshole, and muthafucka in the book. "Have a good night."

"This is some bullshit," she growled. "I told my home-girl you wasn't shit."

Turning to her, I shrugged. "In that case, it's a good thing I'm leaving. Right?"

"Straight up? Lose my fuckin' number."

On a normal day, I considered myself to be a patient man. But she'd definitely tried my patience today. To avoid saying something I'd regret—because I wasn't really an asshole—I opened the door. "Done."

"Wait?" Her tone changed, turned desperate. She grabbed my arm. "Please don't go. Can we talk about it? Finish what we started?"

Not only was Tabatha a liar, she was crazy as hell. Or a narcissist. Or both. "Let's not do this," I said, keeping my voice even.

Once again, she switched up. Now, she was baring teeth. "Fuck you," she yelled, smacking the wall with her palm. "Punk-ass b—"

A door opened behind me, and I wasn't surprised that Tabatha's rage-filled rant had drawn the attention of a neighbor or two. An older man poked his head out. "Is everything alright out here?"

Before I could answer, a flip-flop whizzed by my head, nearly hitting me. "Fine." I ducked when the other shoe flew over my head.

"Go back in your apartment, Daddy. I'm handling this."

Daddy?

"You better handle it, because I have to get up to go to work in the morning," the man said. "I told you about having male company anyway. I'm paying for you to live there."

"Please!" she shouted, pointing at his door. "I'll come see you in a few minutes."

"Bring some food." The man slammed his door.

There was so much wrong with this situation, but I didn't have it in me to ask any questions. Whether the man was her biological father or her sugar daddy, I'd never know.

"Preston?" she called.

I stared at the closed door of her neighbor, then back at her. Without another word, I left her standing there, fury in her eyes.

My phone buzzed yet again when I finally made it to my truck. "What's up, bruh?" I answered.

"Work," Cooper said. "What's the word?"

"Shit. You all packed?" Cooper and I owned Prescott-Hayes Construction. We'd been in business for years and had amassed a small fortune and earned a stellar reputation in Southeast Michigan. Recently, he'd decided to move back to his hometown of Rosewood Heights, South Carolina to help run his family company and be with the woman he loved. While it wasn't an optimal choice, considering our business was busier than ever, I understood his decision. For the first time since I'd known Coop, he was happy. And I was happy for him.

"Almost. Did you see the email from the city? They sent it a few minutes ago."

After I started my car and it connected to Bluetooth, I checked my work account. The approval email was a welcome surprise after the day I'd had. We'd finally received the approval for the condominiums. Construction would start soon. "Just read it," I told him. "Good news."

"Definitely," Coop agreed. "I figure I'll fly back before we break ground."

"Sounds like a plan." I finally pulled out of my parking spot and headed toward I-94. "Remember that woman you met in that bar in Thailand?"

He groaned. "Hell yeah. I still wonder how I got out of that unscathed and injury-free."

I laughed, grateful for the calm before the upcoming storm. "Barely."

Joining the Marine Corps saved my life in many ways. Aside from the occasional field trip or family reunion, my world had pretty much consisted of my block, my school, and my job. While I hadn't been thrilled about enlisting, I'd done it to escape the environment that had once—*and sometimes still did*—felt like a chokehold around my neck. Spending my late teenage years overseas had changed everything for me.

Building a strong brotherhood had played a major role in my transformation from boy to man. Cooper and I had met while we'd both been stationed in Germany. Our backgrounds weren't that similar. He'd grown up the second oldest son of the richest black family in his hometown, and I was the only child of a father who'd died too soon and a mother who'd...lived. But we had one thing in common: anger. Him at his father, and me at mostly everything. Over the years, we'd shared a lot about our lives, from childhood crises to busted relationships. I'd even taken a bullet for him. But he'd saved my life on more than one occasion.

"I just told Angel about that a couple of weeks ago," Coop said.

"I hope you told her the whole truth."

"Every fucked-up part, man. Had her cracking up. Why you thinking about that shit?"

Tabatha's outburst earlier had immediately made me think back to Thailand. Until he'd met Angel and her son Mehki, Coop had consistently made bad choices in women. But LaLa had been the worst. She'd terrorized him from the time we'd landed in Nam Phong to the time we'd departed. "Let's just say, I could've suffered the same fate," I confessed.

"Whoa, bruh. I don't wish that on anyone. I'm telling you…run."

"You know I'm not playin' no games. Had to get the hell up out of her apartment."

He barked out a laugh. "I'm not even gonna lie. I'm glad those days are behind me."

"Me too. Hopefully, your bar fight days are behind you too. Angel is not about that bail money life."

"Damn, you're right about that. I can't even imagine having to explain that to Mehki."

My phone beeped, and I peered at the SYNC display before declining the call. "Shit," I muttered.

"What's up? She chasing you?"

"Nah."

"You might want to take an alternate route. Don't want her to follow your ass home."

I peered out the rearview mirror, his words echoing in my mind. The last thing I needed was a stalker. "I'm good. She's probably fucking her daddy right about now."

"What the hell?"

I shook my head. "You don't want to know," I murmured.

"Where you 'bout to go? Want to shoot some pool?"

My light mood turned dark as thoughts of what I'd find when I reached my destination took over. "On my way to the east side."

"This late?" When I didn't respond, he said, "Alright, man. I know when to change the subject." Coop updated me on the status of the project closeout he was handling while in town. "The client is already talking about hiring us for their next venture," he explained. "We need to go ahead and hire another architect. You've been working nonstop, bruh. You can't be everywhere at once."

Leaving my corporate job as an architect to launch this company had been the best professional decision I'd made. Instead of stuffy board meetings and impossible expectations from firm partners, I had the opportunity to do meaningful work in the community. It helped that Coop and I had the same vision, the same desire to improve life for the residents of my hometown, Detroit.

Over the past several years, we'd expanded the company in ways we hadn't fathomed when we'd first started. Our little company had increased in value, and we'd cultivated a clientele that only brought in more business.

"I'm good with that." I merged onto the expressway. "We definitely need a bigger team. And while we're at it, we can figure out how we want to handle Dave's upcoming retirement."

"I'll have Jackie put a meeting on the calendar to discuss our hiring plans," he offered. "I have a feeling we need to think bigger for staff."

"My schedule is jam-packed next week, but I'll make it work."

A moment later, he asked, "Sure you're good?"

"Fine," was my clipped answer.

Cooper sighed. There wasn't much we didn't know about each other, and he'd been in my life long enough to know why I'd be driving out there this late. "You need me to meet you there?"

"Have you told Dallas about the move yet?" I asked, effectively answering his question without actually telling him no. "It's been over a month since you've been back in Detroit."

Since Cooper had been down south, I'd actually spent

a fair amount of time with Dallas. True to her word, we'd never discussed what had happened in that bathroom at her birthday party. If I was a punk, I probably would've been offended or hurt, but I wasn't trippin' about it. I figured we'd talk at the right time—or never. I certainly wasn't going to question her about it. I'd been through enough to know when to shut the hell up and move on.

"I'll tell her before I leave," he admitted. "Maybe tomorrow. I have a lot of shit to do, and Dallas will slow me down with all of her damn questions."

"If you're worried about PHC, don't."

"Hard not to."

"We already had this discussion, man."

"I heard what you said," he argued, "but executing business remotely is—"

"The same shit people do every damn day," I interrupted. "Look, we have a plan in place, and we're going to work it. You haven't been here since January, and business is still booming."

"I'm just sayin'," he argued. "This is a big change."

"Absolutely. But we're not new to change." Several seconds passed with no conversation. "I told you before that Prescott-Hayes will be ours whether you live in Michigan or South Carolina. *If* you have to be here for anything, you'll get here. Worry about Angel greeting you with open arms."

"Right. But I'm not worried. All I need is permission to stay."

"Alright, man. Let me know if I can help with anything before you hit the road."

"Same. I mean it, bruh."

I had no doubt about that. I thanked him and ended the call. The rest of my forty-five-minute drive was quiet—

no music, no talking. As I sped toward the house I'd once called home, I wondered what I'd find when I got there.

When I arrived, I checked my surroundings, sucked in a deep breath, and made my way to the front door. Using my key, I unlocked it and walked in. The small house was quiet, but the smell of stale air, spoiled food, cigarette smoke, and vomit permeated the air. I flicked the light switch, expecting the lamp to come on, but it didn't. I turned on the overhead light, which had never shined brightly no matter how many electricians I'd hired and expensive light bulbs I'd purchased. Off in the corner, the lamp shade was tipped over, and the thick glass of my late grandmother's favorite lamp was shattered on the floor.

Dirty clothes littered the floor, fast-food bags were piled on the counter, empty pizza boxes sat on the couch. I didn't know why I'd expected anything less than the sight that greeted me. It had always been this way.

My childhood had been spent taking care of home, of her. School had come second; friends or girlfriends hadn't been a priority. Only her. Because I could never trust her to take care of herself or me. While other kids were partying, playing sports, meeting girls, I'd been working so I could make sure we both ate. When it was time to graduate, I'd missed my own graduation because I hadn't wanted to have to explain why she acted the way she did. And when I'd enlisted, I'd spent days reassuring her I'd continue to help her pay the rent.

I walked to the kitchen, grabbed a trash bag from under the sink, and started picking up the trash. When I finished inside, I took the almost-full bag to the garage and checked the '96 Buick. The car keys were on the car seat. Empty beer bottles were strewn on the passenger side and in the back seat. I made quick work cleaning up and tossing the bag into the trash bin.

I glanced at my watch and stepped into the house. I checked each room on my way to the master bedroom, where she was sprawled out on top of a soiled, sheetless mattress. Her clothes were hanging off, her feet were filthy, and her hair was a tangled mess on the top of her head.

"You're here?" Her slurred words were familiar and indicative of her drunken state.

"You called me. At least twenty times in less than an hour."

"I'm so glad you came. Can you grab me a pack of cigarettes from my purse? And a Pepsi. No, a beer." She patted the top of her head. "Shit, my hair is a hot mess. I need to get myself together."

The words *hot* and *mess* were an understatement. I stared down at the first woman I'd ever loved. Kenya Hayes had been a stunner once, so fly that she'd garnered the attention of one of the top modeling agencies. But an unwanted pregnancy at eighteen, a hit-and-run at twenty-one, and a failed marriage had left her with a lot of regrets and an addiction.

I should've felt sad, but all I felt was anger. Disgust, really. Maybe pity. But definitely rage. Because this wasn't the first time I'd had to drop everything and clean up my mother's mess— literally and figuratively. I took a cleansing breath, grabbed the bottle of vodka on the nightstand, and stomped into her bathroom. I heard her struggling outside, screaming at me to stop, but I poured the liquor into the toilet.

"Pres!" she hollered between coughs. "Don't throw out my shit. I paid good money for that."

Sighing, I walked back into the room. "Too late. And

maybe you should've paid the electric bill, or even your cell phone bill, instead of buying a fifth of Tito's."

"Show some respect," she slurred. She picked up her lighter and attempted to light the butt of a cigarette. "I'm still your mother."

"Then act like it, Ma." I snatched the lighter from her. "For once."

"You have no right to talk to me like that, lil' nigga. I will kick your big ass."

I snickered. "Good luck with that."

"You think you're funny." She stood up and nearly fell on her face. When I went to help her, she smacked me. "Don't touch me."

"You can barely stand up."

She shuffled around the room aimlessly, opening drawers, throwing clothes around. I suspected she was looking for her pain pills or her stash of liquor. Because there was always a spare.

I spotted a half-full bottle under the recliner and grabbed it, holding it up. "Looking for this?"

She grabbed the neck of the bottle and tried to snatch it from me, but my firm grip made that impossible in her state. "Give me that shit," she spat.

The unhealthy relationship I had with my mother had taken its toll on me, but it had never stopped me from doing what I had to do—it had never prevented me from succeeding in school and at work, and it had never kept me from being there for her. No matter how exhausting it was, when she called, I came.

Mom shoved me again. "You can get out."

"You know I'm not going to sit here and watch you kill yourself with this drink."

"That's not your decision to make."

Arguing with her about who was in charge wasn't an

option. Because from the time I could think for myself, it felt like I'd been the parent of the relationship. "You called me? What's going on?"

"Shit," she grumbled, pushing papers around on her desk. Eventually, she pulled out an envelope and waved it in front of me. "The mortgage is late, and my water bill is behind. The city is threatening to shut it out…I mean off. The bank wants to foreclose."

I took the envelope from her. "I'll pay both of the bills tomorrow. I told you to just let me handle your finances." It had been a recurring argument between us, because she'd wanted to maintain her independence. Even though that had never stopped her from asking for money.

"So you can give me an allowance?" she questioned. "Hell no."

I let out a heavy sigh. "Why don't you take a shower? I'll change your sheets and throw these clothes in the washing machine."

She smiled for the first time since I'd arrived. "Can you go to the store and grab me a couple of candy bars?" My mother loved chocolate. "I ran out."

"I'll take care of it."

Mom tried to take the bottle from me again, but I was quicker. She glared at me as I poured that one out too. "When you leave, I'll just get more." Her matter-of-fact response irritated me. "You always think you're better than me," she growled.

"Nah, that's not it. I think *you're* better than *this*," I yelled. "Damn, Ma, when is it going to be enough? When are you going to start taking responsibility for yourself? When are you going to get tired of living like this?" I waved my hands around the room. "Nothing has changed. You're still living in the same place, talking about the same shit, and fucking around with the same people."

"See?" She pointed at me. "You're just like your father."

"Don't do that." It was her patented response every time I told her she needed to get her shit together. Soon, the tears would follow.

Her chin trembled and the first tear fell. "He treated me like I was beneath him too."

My parents had been children themselves when I was conceived, and their short-lived marriage had fizzled out before my third birthday. There'd been no co-parenting, no communication between them. Just bitterness on my mother's part. But I'd seen my father every other weekend and on the occasional holiday until he'd died, right before my thirteenth birthday.

"Don't start this," I warned. "Dad isn't here anymore, and I don't want to talk about this shit. I've heard it my whole life."

"That's what you think," she said with a shrug.

I froze. "What are you talking about?"

"Since you think you know everything, I'm going to tell you something you don't know."

Frustrated, I snapped, "What? What is it I don't know?"

"Preston Hayes Sr. was not your father. Your real father lived his best life—without you." She stumbled into the bathroom, whirling around to face me. "Now, run tell that." Then, she slammed the door in my face.

Chapter Three

SLIDE

Dallas

If I didn't like dick so much, I would've sworn off men a long time ago. Because what the hell else were they good for? Surely not financial security, because I could pay my own bills. Definitely not protection, because the last few men I'd dated had been so damn weak. More scared of spiders than I was, and certainly not willing to get my back in any fight. Absolutely not conversation, because they didn't listen. And they were so damn needy. Always wanting time and checking in and phone calls. I didn't have time for that shit.

Case in point…my client. Langston Sykes was the son of a prominent politician. Our families had traveled in the same circles for years. His mother was like an angel on earth, a beautiful woman with a genuine spirit. Too bad her son was a self-entitled asshole who cared more about his fingernails than about people. On paper, though, he was the perfect man. Educated. Handsome. Successful. But he was a little punk. Instead of killing the bee that had flown into my office, he'd walked out and asked Dexter to come in and do it. And for the last hour and a half, he'd nitpicked on every clause in the prenuptial I'd been negotiating with his future wife. The jerk had insisted on weight and BMI criteria for his fiancée, had suggested adding a required amount of sex per week to the agreement, had requested limits to social media posts, and had even tried to sneak in a section giving him the leeway to cheat once a year with no questions.

"Anything else I should be thinking about?" He glanced at his watch. For most of our meeting, he'd failed to make eye contact, splitting his attention between the floor, his phone, and my breasts. "My colleague's brother mentioned it might be wise to include a beauty budget—because, you know…women spend thousands on plastic surgery nowadays, and I don't want to pay for that shit."

I blinked. I'd never liked him, but I loved his mother, which was why I'd agreed to this *favor*. Now, I was just ready for this to be over.

He shrugged. "She'll sign it. I'm a catch. She should be lucky I chose her."

"Sure!" My pseudo enthusiasm dripped with sarcasm. "While we're at it, how about we add in a drug test requirement? Better yet, how about we put in a clause regulating the number of orgasms she can have when she masturbates?"

He leaned back in his chair and crossed his legs. "I think I like that drug test provision. I hear she did ecstasy back in the day." When I didn't respond, he continued, "Really?" His amused smile made me sick. "Is this how we're treating clients now?"

I was done with Langston. If he didn't know it now, he

would in a few minutes. When we were younger, my siblings had *affectionately* nicknamed me I.Q., for Ice Queen. Or D.D., for *Damn, Dallas!*" Which often was accompanied by "you're so damn evil." Early on, I'd decided no one should know what I was thinking or how I felt at any given time—unless I wanted them to know. Not only had I mastered the art of the poker face, but my "you ain't shit" stare had weakened even the strongest men. I wouldn't say I was mean, but I didn't necessarily like people. I fucked with my family—and my *two and a possible.* That was the number of friends on my list—Demi, Cooper, and… sorta Preston.

I met his gaze, narrowing my eyes on him. "No. This is how *I'm* treating *you.*" Under normal circumstances and with clients who didn't try to get me to play Hide and Go Get It with them as kids, I would've never taken it there. But Langston? I didn't give a fuck about him or his micropenis. Yeah, women talked, but so did money. And he had a lot of it.

Langston cleared his throat. "You haven't changed, Dallas. You're still a bitch."

"Thanks. I'll be that for you." I processed a refund of his retainer and fed the contents of his file into my paper shredder.

"Maybe you should think about who you're talking to. I'm not the same boy you grew up with."

"You look the same to me. Sound the same too. Lame. Let's not pretend to like each other anymore for the sake of our parents." Folding my arms, I stood. "Find another attorney."

Langston frowned. "You can't do this. I paid you."

"And I refunded you," I said with a shrug. "We're all set here."

"I need this done," he argued.

"Hire someone who'll do it."

"Look, I'm sorry. You know I was just playing with you. We've known each other for years. We have history." He stepped forward, reaching out to grab my hand. "You—"

"Don't touch me," I warned. "And don't bother making up a lie to your mother. I'll be sure to tell her myself that you're full of shit."

After a long pause, he apparently thought better of arguing with me, because he simply nodded and left the office without another word.

Closing my eyes, I let out a slow, cleansing breath before I made my way to the window. On the street, I could see Langston practically running to his car. I also noticed a photographer in front of the building next door. *I hate this.*

Sometime ago, a few of my siblings and I had the bright idea to combine our resources and purchase an office building. My parents were entrepreneurs, operating several successful businesses. All of us had followed their lead. It just made sense to have a central location, where we could see clients, work our own businesses, and collaborate with each other.

Located in Ann Arbor, the spacious building had nine office suites, one for each sibling and an extra for guests. Currently, Dexter, Bliss, Blake, and I worked there every day. We called the space "Young Haven." It didn't matter what happened throughout the day—knowing that at least one of my siblings was around made all the difference. It was one of my safe places. Now, I had to worry about strange people camped outside my place of work. And I didn't like that.

A few minutes later, Dex poked his head in my office. "Took you long enough." He stepped inside and sat on the small sofa near the window. "Now I owe Blake money. I thought he wouldn't last thirty minutes."

I shrugged, joining him on the couch. "I really tried. But…just no. Not all money is good money."

He gave me a fist bump. "Exactly. Mom called. She wants us to be at the field early for a family meeting."

"About?"

"Shit, I don't know. I just show up."

"Fine." Resting my head on his shoulder, I said, "Did you see that Keisha T vlog about me?"

Since Kimball had tilted my world on its axis, I'd been followed by random people wherever I went and received threatening messages from obsessed fans. And my inbox was inundated with interview requests from wannabe reporters. Speculation about my life and my character had become fodder for news outlets looking for a story and lyin'-ass vloggers vying for clicks. Which definitely didn't make a potential political campaign viable. The latest video was a "documentary" about my love life and the slew of men I'd left heartbroken.

"I saw that shit," he grumbled. "I want to know where that loud-ass Keisha T even found those people to interview. I was watching it like, who the hell is that? Talking about they 'grew up with you' and had 'inside knowledge.' Da fuq?"

I laughed. "Right? I'd never even seen those people before. And the one chick who said we hung out together in college? I met her one time at a party." I only remembered that encounter after Demi had refreshed my memory. We'd met the woman at a party, and she'd said two words to me. "*Hey, girl.*" That's it. How that translated to her being my former friend, I had no idea.

"Yeah, I remember her too. She tried to get with me a few times." Dex and I had chosen to buck tradition and go to an out-of-state college. We'd both attended Hampton University for our undergraduate degrees. It had been scary as shit leaving the comfort of our hometown, but having him and Demi there had made all the difference. I knew without a doubt, I wouldn't be the woman I was today if I hadn't experienced HBCU life. "Did she even graduate?"

"I have no idea," I murmured.

"Are you okay?" There was something about Dexter's voice, the way he was, that made me feel secure enough to be vulnerable with him. He had a calm demeanor, spoke in a soft tone, and never overtalked anyone. He was a magnet and people wanted to talk to him, to confide in him. He was the gentleman talking to the shy person in the corner and boosting their confidence to work the room. It was a superpower, really, and the reason why he was successful in his career as a professional wingman. A relationship coach. A real-life *Hitch*. While Bliss matched people with their potential soulmates, Dex helped his clients approach potential partners—among other services. And he made a great living at it.

I shrugged. "If I said I was, would you believe me?"

"No, but I wouldn't push you."

Opening myself up to share bits and pieces about myself to anyone—including my siblings—had always been hard for me. I'd always loved that my family allowed me the space to come to them when I was ready. It was the benefit of being the offspring of Stewart and Victoria Young. In hindsight, I realized their habit of letting us set the rules of conversation had been intentional. They'd encouraged us to think about the right time to speak, what we needed to say, and how we wanted to say it. They'd also taught us the power of acceptance, of community, of trust, of love.

After a moment passed, I finally looked at Dex. "When Maya approached me about her plan, I didn't know what to think. I didn't even realize I wanted it. The possibility that this shit with Kimball could derail my future career prospects is pretty messed up. I feel like I got caught slipping or something. Like everything I've worked for or want to achieve is in jeopardy."

He squeezed my hand. "That's not true. Your accomplishments are yours. This doesn't change that. Maya hasn't mentioned it yet. Let's not assume the organization cares about some dumb vloggers who don't know anything about you. Focus on your brunch with the board of directors."

"You know it's not that simple."

"Yes, it is. Dallas, you got this. I'm not worried, and neither is anyone else who knows you."

"That's the problem. The board doesn't know me. Suddenly, people are analyzing my dating history, passing judgment on my choices, and assuming I fuck anybody with a dick."

He chuckled. "Even if you did, it's nobody's business."

"I didn't," I clarified. Despite my love of sex, I was very careful about who I let in my space. Most men need not apply. "I don't. But it's the type of first impression that's hard to overcome."

"Hey. I love you regardless of your 'ho-ish ways,' and they will too."

I cracked up. "Shut up." The jokes my family had cracked during Blake's housewarming had been epic. I couldn't be angry they'd laughed at my expense—once they knew I was okay, of course. Even my parents had gotten in on the fun.

"Seriously, though. He's a punk-ass muthafucka. Remind me why I didn't fuck him up last week again?"

"Because that wouldn't solve anything." I knew my brothers were itching to beat the crap out of Kimball. Violence was not the answer. "And Blake called dibs," I added with a giggle.

"I don't know. Blake's on her 'the world is better with love' tip lately. Besides, he'll hear it better from me."

"You better not let her hear you say that."

"I'll say it to her face." He stood, tugging me to my feet as well. "She's getting soft. Let's go get food before our game."

Feeling better, I grabbed my purse and followed my brother out. And prayed I could enjoy the rest of my day without another false headline making the news.

"DAMN, DALLAS!" my brother, Tristan, grumbled from behind me. "That's two strikes."

Frustrated at my lack of prowess on the field today, I had half a mind to toss my bat at him and walk away. Figured I'd have an off day when my most competitive and irritating sibling had decided to play. Softball was one of our favorite pastimes. Ever since we were little kids, our parents had insisted we learn the game and play competitively. And we'd never stopped, forming an adult co-ed team every summer and fall.

I glared at Tristan over my shoulder. "I don't need a reminder." Turning my attention back to the pitcher, I swung the bat a couple of times, then took my stance. I glanced at my father, who was peering at me from third base. On first base, my niece Raven was stretching. And my younger brother, Asa, was chatting with the woman playing short stop for the opposing team. Bases loaded. Bottom of the seventh inning. It was up to me.

The pitcher narrowed his eyes on me, drew back, and tossed the ball my way. It only took a second, but when my bat hit the ball, I didn't stop to think. I just ran. I sprinted past first base, then second. I could hear my brothers yelling commands, but I kept going. My mother's strongly-worded order to stop didn't permeate either, and I sailed past third. To my left, I saw the ball flying toward home base. And I went down, sliding into home before the catcher tagged me.

"Safe!" the umpire shouted.

Pain radiated up my leg to my hip. I rolled onto my back, struggling to catch my breath. "Shit," I whispered. And since I couldn't say anything else, I continued to say that until my heart rate slowed down.

A moment later, I heard my name. When I opened my eyes, I saw Dex standing above me. Tristan, Asa, and my mom joined him shortly after.

"Dallas?" my mom called. She was five foot two, shorter than all of us, but she always seemed tall. Probably because she radiated confidence, commanded any room she entered.

I cracked one eye open. "Yes?"

"Oh, Lord. She's hurt. Asa, go get some ice." With concerned eyes, she bent low and touched my forehead with the back of her hand. "Are you okay, babe?"

"No," I whined. "Not okay. But I don't have a fever, Mom."

Dex laughed. "Exactly."

"Quiet." Mom smacked him. "It's a habit." She squeezed my ankle.

When she rubbed my hip bone, I cried out, "Ouch."

"You'll probably have a bruise," she mused.

"Suck it up, sis," Tristan said. "Walk it off. She's fine," he argued, nudging my other leg with his shoe.

I wanted to kick him, but I could barely lift my leg. *What the hell was I thinking, acting all eighteen and shit?* Yet, even as sore as I was, I managed to punch Tristan in his shin. "Shut the hell up."

It was just like my oldest brother to blow off my injury. He never let a little pain keep him from running or playing football or doing anything. And he expected the same from us. Bruised knee? Get over it. Stubbed toe? That's nothing. Broken arm? It'd heal. When we were kids, he'd acted like a damn taskmaster, forcing us to do push-ups in the rain, making us run laps around the block for no reason, and assigning chores to do around the house when our parents put him in charge. Ugh. That's why we all called him the *fun killer*, because he could spot fun from a mile away and ruin it.

"Leave your sister alone," Mom said. "She gave us a W."

My father appeared a few seconds later. "What's up?" He glanced down at me and motioned at Dex. "Pick her up."

Dex did as he was told, scooping me up and carrying me into the dugout. Luckily, it was one of those perfect summer days. A light breeze cooled everything off, and the sun was still shining. After I'd graduated from Hampton, I'd considered moving to the DMV area permanently. But I knew I'd miss Michigan. It was home.

"Thanks," I told Dex when he set me on the bench.

Blake sat next to me. "You okay?" She sipped from her bottle of water. "Because I love you, I won't post the video I took of your dramatic slide into home to my Insta."

I leaned my head back, resting it on the wall. I was so focused on my goal that I hadn't even thought about how I must've looked out there. "It was bad, huh?"

She snickered. "Yeah, sis. I don't know if you even realized you were screaming your ass off. Jersey riding up, titties swangin'." She barked out a laugh. "Next time, tuck your neck in and raise your arms."

I studied the angry bruise forming on my arm. "This shit hurts."

Bliss stepped into the dugout. "Forgot this in the car." She held up a first aid kit, sat down, and started tending to me. "You kicked ass out there, Sissy."

I looked at Blake. "See? I did good."

Blake shrugged. "Yes. You still looked crazy as hell, though."

Giggling, Bliss nodded. "You did. But you did your thing."

"You both get on my damn nerves," I said.

A few minutes later, my father called us out onto the grass. Dex once again helped me get there. Once we were all situated, Dad cleared his throat. "Since some of you are incapable of being on time for anything—" he shot Blake an accusatory glare, "—your mother and I want to take this time to talk to you about the retreat next month."

The Annual *Young in Love* Couples Retreat was in its 25th year. Each weekend event was full of seminars on everything from love languages to sex. Couples consistently ranked the experience high and referred others. The wait-list was long, but my parents were committed to the work. We tagged along every year, and afterward, we'd go on a family vacation. It was the highlight of the year for most of us.

"There's been a change of plans," Dad continued. "We had an amazing year. Business ventures, job offers, new romances, and one more grandbaby."

My mother took over. "Initially, we thought it'd be fun to stay up north for the family vacation, which is perfect for us and something we all enjoy. However, your father and I felt the need to step it up a little, to celebrate every single one of our wins. The retreat will still take place in August, but we're going to move the family vacation to September. We've decided to charter a yacht and sail the Mediterranean. Our treat."

"Whoa!" Asa said, his eyes wide and his mouth hanging open. "Are you serious?"

"Do we lie?" was my father's response.

Asa ducked his head. "No," he grumbled.

"Since it's our fortieth wedding anniversary, we'd like to renew our wedding vows with all of you present," my father told us.

"Paityn and Duke are already on board," my mother chimed in, referring to my older sister and my brother, who both lived out of state. Paityn, in Cali with her husband; and Duke, in Atlanta being Duke.

"We'll be finalizing all the details in the next few days," Dad added. "The only thing you need to do is tell me who you're bringing and pack."

"Love you," Mom said, before she and my dad said their goodbyes and left.

Twenty minutes later, I limped into our favorite hangout, The Ice Box. While Dex and Lennox grabbed a table, I hobbled to the bathroom with Blake. On my way out, I spotted Preston at the bar.

"Oh, there's Preston." Blake headed toward him, but I gripped her wrist.

"Hold on," I told my sister. "I'm not sure I want him to know I'm here." I did look a hot mess after all, in my baseball cap and dusty softball team uniform.

"Girl, please." She waved a dismissive hand my way. "It's just Preston. If you haven't fucked him again by now, I doubt it's going to happen."

Under normal circumstances, I'd agree. It was *just*

Preston. But that *sex*uation hadn't been normal. *One night. One fuck.* That mantra had been plastered to my bathroom mirror for me to see every damn day since our hot bathroom romp. For the most part, my *fuck*irmation worked. After all, I excelled at compartmentalization. And I purposefully used other people as buffers. Because despite all my bravado, I wasn't confident I could be alone with him and not want a repeat. Or a *three*peat.

As if she read my mind, Blake tucked a strand of my hair behind my ear and wiped my cheek. "You're still fly. Grass in your hair and all."

I rolled my eyes, patting my hair down as if that would help.

"He looks a little down, though," Blake offered.

Turning, I took a moment to study him. My sister was right. From where I stood, I couldn't see his face, but I did notice his slumped posture. It wasn't like Preston to slouch, and I'd never known him to drink alone. "Give me a sec," I told Blake. I shuffled over to him, wincing every time my left foot touched the hard floor. My body ached everywhere. Instead of coming to the bar, I should've taken my ass home to soak in the tub.

When I made it to the bar, I peered over at him. He didn't even look up. He just sat there quietly, staring at the drink in front of him. Unmoving. Solemn.

The bartender walked over to me. "What can I get you?"

I glanced at Preston again and made a decision to try to make him laugh. So, I said, "I'll have a margarita, light on the ice, heavy on the Patrón."

Preston looked up then, his dark, sad gaze meeting mine.

I winked at him and was pleasantly surprised when the corner of his mouth quirked up. I grinned at him, then turned to the bartender. Pointing to Preston, I said, "I think he's paying. Right?"

Preston's low chuckle settled something in my stomach. "Right. Put it on my tab."

I sat on the bar stool next to him. Slowly. "And keep them coming."

Chapter Four

COME THROUGH

Preston

"I'm waiting…"

"I'm still not telling you." I laughed when she folded her arms over her chest and pouted. "No matter how many times you ask me."

Dallas smacked her palm on the bar top. "Really?"

I glanced over at Dallas, raking my gaze over every inch of her. Even though she had grass in her hair and wore a dirty softball uniform, she still managed to redirect my thoughts from my fucked-up life to my dick. "Really," I confirmed.

"Fine. If you won't tell me what Cooper wants to talk to me about, I'll leave it alone."

"Good." For the last several minutes, we'd gone back and forth about Cooper and his *news*. And every time she'd formulated an argument designed to convince me to reveal all, I'd told her the same thing—no.

She sighed. "He's not answering my calls. Is it bad?"

I laughed. "I'm not answering that."

"It's bad." She tapped her fingernails on the bar. "Is Angel pregnant?"

I shot her a sidelong glance. "What?"

"Is he sick or something?" was her next question.

"Dallas?"

"Huh?"

"Stop. You need to talk to Cooper about Cooper. Not me."

She propped her elbow on the bar and rested her chin on her palm. Sighing, she said, "I'm going to kill him. I told him not to fuck up. And he went and did just that. Then, he came home and promptly dropped off the grid. It's been over a month."

"Aren't you supposed to be eating dinner with your family?" I asked, glancing back at her group.

Over in the corner, several of her siblings were laughing and eating together. Since she'd been sitting with me, some of them had come over and kicked it for a moment or two before rejoining the big group. But she hadn't even attempted to go over there with them.

Dallas looked back too. She shrugged. "They're alright." She took her second shot of the night and motioned to my glass. "Are you going to drink that?"

I stared down at my still-full first shot glass. The revelation that my dad wasn't my father and my mother had lied about it for almost forty years had wreaked havoc in my life. For the past few days, I'd gone over every detail of my childhood, reliving unpleasant memories in an attempt to make sense out of everything.

After my mom had dropped that bomb on me, she'd closed herself off in her bathroom. To avoid tearing the door off at its hinges, I'd left her there. I hadn't spoken to her since. Not because I hadn't called her, but because she'd never answered. I'd driven to her house after work today, and she hadn't been home. Instead of sitting at my place, wondering and worrying about her whereabouts, I'd come here. Partly to escape my thoughts, but mostly to prove to myself I wasn't anything like her.

Ordering this shot was an exercise in willpower, one I'd performed many times. The good news was I could never bring myself to take the drink. I couldn't use the same coping mechanism my mother had used all of my life. I didn't need it to feel something—or nothing.

My relationship with alcohol was complicated. Sure, I enjoyed a beer with my homeboys every now and then. And I didn't mind taking a shot of tequila or having Jameson with my cigar. But drinking just to be drinking was not my thing. I'd seen the effects of addiction on someone's life. I had a firsthand seat to the destruction too much liquor could cause, and I didn't want that for myself—or anyone I loved.

"Hey?"

I closed my eyes. Dallas' voice was like balm on dry, cracked skin. Soothing, soft. I felt her eyes on me, watching me, *seeing* me. Still, I couldn't face her; I didn't want to show her even a glimpse of the turmoil I knew would be swimming in my eyes. It was best to keep that to myself, to hide that part of my life from her.

"Preston?" she called again.

"What?" I murmured, keeping my gaze trained on my glass.

She placed her hand on top of mine and squeezed. "You… Um. You… Shit."

Unable to help myself, I peered over at her. Dallas was many things. But she was never someone who stumbled over her words. The fact that she was having a hard time articulating amused me. It also intrigued me.

She blew out a quick breath. "So... Yeah. I know we don't really..." She covered her forehead with her hand and muttered something incoherent. "What I'm trying to say is...you can talk to me. If you want to," she added under her breath.

I barked out a laugh. The words were good, and I believed she was sincere, but the delivery sucked.

Dallas shoved me. "Don't laugh at me. I'm serious."

I searched her eyes. "I know."

She smirked, drawing my attention to the dimple on her right cheek. Dallas was a beautiful woman. It didn't matter if she wore jeans and a T-shirt, a business suit, a dress, or a ripped, dusty softball uniform. Smooth brown skin. Large expressive eyes. Curvaceous hips. Despite my best efforts to appear unaffected by her, I usually failed. Because I always wanted to kiss her, to touch her, to hold her.

That night in October had done nothing to dampen my desire for her. In fact, it'd only made every woman who'd come after her pale in comparison. And it wasn't just the sex—which was definitely unforgettable. It was just her.

Over the years, I'd dated many different types of women. Some older than me, others younger than me. Women who loved sports, ladies who loved the ballet. Women who worked corporate jobs and women who worked on the assembly line at an automotive plant. Dallas ran circles around all of them. She was consistent, intentional, honest. Always thinking, always moving. Never stagnant. She spoke her mind, and she knew when to be quiet—sometimes. I knew what I was going to get with her. I also knew I could trust her, even if she didn't think she could trust me.

"You look…" She licked her bottom lip. "You're sad."

I wasn't surprised she'd recognized the sadness. She'd grown up with parents who studied and taught the human mind. Many of her siblings had followed in their footsteps and had become therapists. Although Dallas didn't work in the field, she'd majored in psychology in undergrad.

"Yeah," I admitted, shocking myself.

"I meant what I said, you know? I'm here to listen, if you want to talk."

Talk. Listen. The words were simple but loaded at the same time. She was offering me a lifeline, but I wasn't sure I could use it. In the end, I decided not to. "Thanks, but I don't want to think about it."

"Okay." She waved the bartender over and ordered onion rings. Glancing at me, she grinned. "What? I'm hungry now and I deserve fried food."

I chuckled. "Because you played softball?"

"Hell yeah. And I won the game."

I gave her a high-five. "Alright. Is there any footage?"

She winced visibly. "No comment."

"Uh-oh. Let me guess, one of your siblings took a video."

Dallas picked up her glass of water and gulped it down. "No comment," she repeated.

"Hey, Sissy." Blake joined us at the bar. "We're about to head out. Lennox has a speech to write."

"Damn." Dallas' shoulders fell. "I ordered onion rings."

"You're just now ordering food?" Lennox asked, approaching us. He looked at his watch. "It's late."

"It's a treat," Dallas said. "For saving *your* ass in that

game today, brotha Lennox. Since you nearly lost us the game by striking out."

"Um, ma'am," Blake said. "Don't come for my man."

"Matter of fact," Dallas continued, "I was so distracted by the pain shooting down my leg that I forgot we'd placed a side wager on this game. I think you owe me some money, Professor." She did the cabbage patch dance, then mimicked a mic drop. "Boom!"

I covered my mouth, once again amused by the woman sitting next to me. She really was a breath of fresh air. I'd been around the Young family many times. Barbecues, events, birthday parties. Every single time, they'd treated me like I was part of their clan. Being the only child, I appreciated that.

Lennox groaned and slapped a fifty-dollar bill on the bar top. "You got me. Dinner on me."

Dallas picked up the bill, held it up to the light, and stuffed it in her pocket. "Thanks. Next time, double or nothing."

Yawning, Blake asked, "Can you get those onion rings to go? Dex left with some chick, and Tristan? He disappeared like he always does. And you know Asa. He ain't taking nobody home. So, we're dropping you off."

Dallas opened her mouth to speak. "I—"

"I'll take her," I offered.

Dallas blinked.

Blake placed her palm under her sister's chin and pushed her mouth closed. "Thanks, Preston." She patted my shoulder, then whispered something in Dallas' ear. She cracked up when Dallas pushed her away.

"Get your ass out of here, heffa," Dallas grumbled through clenched teeth.

Curious, I asked, "What's up?"

Blake smirked. "She's—"

Dallas covered her sister's mouth. "She's leaving. Bye, Blake."

Lennox and Blake said their goodbyes and walked away.

We sat there in silence for a moment before Dallas turned to me. "My sister talks too much."

"What did she say?"

"Nothing," she chirped. "Never mind."

Several minutes later, the bartender set a plate of onion rings in front of her and the bottle of ketchup. She immediately picked a ring up and bit into it, groaning with delight.

"Good, huh?" I asked.

She gestured toward her plate. "Want one? They're delicious."

"No, thanks."

"I wish I knew how to cook. I would make these all the time." She dipped another onion ring into her ketchup. "When Duke comes to town, I always bribe him to do it."

A couple of months ago, I went with Dallas to her brother's couples cooking class. I found out then just how untalented she was in the kitchen. The steak had been so tough, I'd had to stop and get something else to eat on my way home. "Have you thought about learning to do it yourself?"

She paused, onion ring midair. Glancing at me out of the corner of her eye, she shook her head. "Hell no. That's what chefs are for, right?"

I laughed. "You're a trip."

"We've already established that cooking is not my gift. The most I can do is cut up vegetables, because I was always early to help my mother cook for Thanksgiving. That damn Blake purposely came late so she wouldn't have to peel the potatoes for the potato salad." Dallas continued munching on her food and talking about random shit, like celery and green peppers. She'd gone through all the ingredients of her mother's famous potato salad and was now telling me she'd tried to sneak pre-cooked boiled eggs into her mom's house one year. "Mom made me go to the store and buy more. I had to peel all those mugs too. I hate that."

"Is there anything you can cook?" I wondered aloud.

"Oh, yeah. I can bake chicken. Oh, and I can make rice—" she covered her face, "—in the rice cooker?" I didn't realize I was smiling until she said, "Why are you smiling? 'Cause I'm pitiful?"

Because you're beautiful. "Not even a little bit," I told her.

"Do you cook?" she asked, pouring more ketchup on her plate. "I mean, I've known you for years and—"

"We really don't know each other," I finished for her.

A moment passed. "Maybe we should do better?"

"I'm ready if you are."

"Is this awkward for you?" she asked.

The question threw me off, but I quickly recovered. "How so?"

"That we're sitting here by ourselves, learning things about each other we never bothered to learn before."

I leaned closer and whispered, "Why is that?"

Her gaze dropped to my lips. "We had sex."

Dallas had this uncanny ability to catch me off guard. I wasn't expecting her to bring up Halloween, but talking about that instead of my personal shit was better any day. "We did."

"Yeah, but before that, we didn't really have much alone time."

"By design?"

She eyed me skeptically. "Maybe." She hitched a shoulder. "I don't know. But just so we're clear, I don't want to talk about it now, either."

I laughed again. "Tell me how you really feel."

"I just did."

"You brought it up, though."

"Only because I wanted to say something else."

"Something else that has nothing to do with sex?"

"Not exactly." She stretched a bit. "I'm going to be stiff. You might have to help me off this stool."

"Still sore from that game-winning slide into home base?"

She snickered. "Very. I'm never doing that shit again. Anyway, I brought it up because we're alone now. The last time we were alone, we got busy."

"I recall that night a little differently."

Arching a brow, she said, "What is your recollection?"

"We had an unspoken conversation and decided to explore an avenue."

"That's one way to put it."

"Then you said we wouldn't talk about it again," I continued.

"And you agreed."

"I didn't say anything that night. *You* set the rules."

Dallas placed her hands in her lap. "Did you want to talk about it?"

"*Talk* is not really the right word, Dallas."

"What is the right word, then?"

"Repeat," I said.

She sucked in a deep breath, then stood. "It's time to go." She started to shuffle away but stopped. "I meant it's time for *me* to go home and *you* to go to your house. With no detours to the bathroom."

With a smirk, I nodded. "Whatever you want."

During the short drive to Dallas' house, we didn't talk

much. But it was just as well. As much as I'd enjoyed my time with her, I knew it wouldn't last. Dallas' ability to compartmentalize her emotions and feelings was only rivaled by one person—me. I understood what was at play here. And I would respect her wish to keep things distant.

"Thanks for helping me up these steps." Dallas unlocked her front door and opened it. "Tonight was alright, Preston. I had a good time, even though my hip is on fire from sitting on that barstool." She stepped inside her house and kicked off her shoes. "I really need to take a bath."

Am I supposed to go in with her? The fact that she was still talking to me, and not closing the door in my face, prompted me to follow her inside. "Do you need anything?" I shut the door behind me.

She glanced at me over her shoulder. "Only if you got those healing hands." She let out a cute giggle and lowered herself to a chair. "Just kidding. All I need is a good soak."

I tried to recall if I'd ever been inside her home without a buffer. *Nope.* The architect in me had catalogued the design elements of the house, the wall color, the trim, the type of doors she had, the thickness of the dark hardwood flooring, the open flow from the living room to the kitchen. But I'd never really paid attention to the décor, the tiny pieces of herself displayed around the room, the pictures of those she loved placed on shelves. I picked up a small picture of her, Duke, and Dexter—The Triples, as I'd heard them called before. In it, Dallas was in the middle, flanked by her brothers. Protected. It looked like they might've been at a picnic or something, because they were dressed casually, and Duke had a basketball in his free hand. I'd watched her and Coop with their respective siblings. It always felt like I'd missed something important in my own life, something valuable, something priceless.

Wasting time on "what-ifs" had never been my thing, but now that I knew I had a different father, I couldn't help but wonder if I had siblings out there somewhere.

"Still don't want to talk about it?" she asked.

I caught Dallas' pained look when I met her gaze. "Maybe you should take some Advil or Aleve?" I suggested.

She rested her leg on the ottoman. "I'm okay. Are you?"

I sighed, torn between telling her everything and telling her nothing. Earlier, she'd effectively doused my hope for a repeat when she'd ended our conversation, which was okay. But I couldn't help but wonder why I was there.

A knock on the front door pulled me out of my thoughts.

"Oh, shit. Who the hell is that?" She struggled to get up from her chair. I helped her up. "Thanks," she murmured, walking to the door slowly. "Coop!" she shouted when she opened the door. She smacked him. "I said I would kick your ass on sight, but I'm too happy you're not dead from alcohol poisoning."

I grinned, grateful Coop had finally come to tell her his news. I gave him dap. "I'm glad you came by, man. I was tired of the interrogation."

Coop thanked me for not telling his business. Then, he glanced at Dallas, then me, then back at Dallas. I could tell his mind was running with the possibilities. "What are you doing at Dallas' house anyway?" he asked.

"Leaving." She nudged me out the door. The bubble we'd been in had finally burst, which I'd expected. And knowing Dallas, she wouldn't want anyone to think there was more going on here than it was. Especially since I knew she'd been dealing with PR issues.

Cooper narrowed his eyes, studying both of us.

"Right." He crossed his arms. "Listen, I can't stay, but I wanted to tell you in person. I'm moving to Rosewood Heights. Tonight."

Dallas' eyes widened and a slow smile spread across her lips. "Because you're in love with Angel." When Cooper confirmed her suspicion, she cheered. "I knew it!" She pulled him into a hug, then smacked him again. "That's for planning a move to a whole 'nother state without telling me. You're lucky Charleston is a short flight away. Punk."

Cooper smiled. I'd never seen my best friend so happy, and considering what he'd been through, I thought it was about time. "Thank you, Dallas," he said. "You were right."

"I'm right 99.999% of the time," Dallas said with a shrug.

"Yeah, I'm not agreeing to that." Coop told us he had to go and assured Dallas he'd leave his phone on. He gave her another hug and me another dap. Before he left, he reminded me of our conference call next Monday. I wished him luck, and Dallas and I watched him hop in his truck and drive away.

Then, I was alone with Dallas again, only this time I was standing outside the door. "I need to get going," I told her.

She slipped her hand in mine and tugged, stopping my retreat. "Wait."

I peered at her, wanting nothing more than to tuck that errant strand of her hair behind her ear. "Yes?"

Stepping close to me, so close I could smell the hint of her soap, so close I could rest my forehead on hers, she said, "I hope I was able to keep your mind off your troubles." She searched my face, smoothed her thumb over mine. "Sometimes life happens so fast, you just need to slow it down. It helps to think about everything else but what's weighing you down."

I stared down at her sincere eyes. Sitting with me alone, talking about random shit, joking… That wasn't Dallas. At least, that wasn't the Dallas *I* knew. The realization that she'd completely stepped out of her own comfort zone for me made me want to pull her closer, to carry her inside. But I knew that couldn't happen right now. Instead, I nodded. "Thank you." Saying anything more wasn't an option. While I wanted to share with her what had happened, I didn't think it was wise to bare my soul tonight. "Take some meds. I hope you feel better."

"I'll get there. I have no choice. You don't either."

"Right."

She gave me a hug. Damn, she felt good, she felt right. I allowed myself to sink into the embrace, burying my nose in her hair and letting her hold me for as long as she wanted to. I needed this. I needed someone calm, someone strong.

Eventually, and all too soon, she pulled away. Smiling, she whispered, "Drive safe, Preston."

I hesitated, because I didn't want to walk away from this. Dallas hadn't said anything to indicate tonight was anything more than a friend helping a friend, but it felt different. It felt like we'd crossed a line. It was more than bathroom sex, deeper than a quick fuck.

Unable to stop myself, I reached out and brushed my thumb over her cheek. "Dallas," I murmured.

She sucked in a deep breath. "Yes?"

I probably could've asked to stay, but I wouldn't. When or if I spent the night with Dallas, she would have to initiate it. "Thanks," I whispered. A moment later, I backed away, waved at her, and headed to my truck. As I drove home, her words replayed in my mind. Dallas was right. My time to wallow was up. I was thankful for the small reprieve from my inner turmoil, for the time we'd spent together. It had helped more than words could say. Tomorrow, I'd start working through it and figuring everything out.

Chapter Five

PICK UP YOUR FEELINGS

Dallas

"Can we stop now?" I bent low, hands on my knees, gasping for breath.

"No, we can't," Paityn chirped.

I peered up at my now-jogging-in-place sister, who looked like she'd just stepped off the runway with her soft, short curls and cute outfit. "You're killing me." I coughed. *Damn, why can't I breathe*?

"Obviously, you need to work out, Sissy." Tyn stretched before segueing into a set of lunges. "What happened to you?"

"I knew I should've stayed my ass home." I glared at my big sister. Paityn had business in town and had flown in yesterday evening. She was a sight for sore, tired eyes. And since she'd come without her husband, Bishop, she'd decided to stay with me instead of my parents' house. Blake and Bliss had come over, and we'd had a little slumber party. Just what I needed. *Sister time.* We'd spent the night catching up, laughing at each other and everyone else, eating Paityn's good cooking, and strengthening our already tight bond. But now? She could get the hell up out of here with her "let's go for a run" self.

"Come on, slow poke." Tyn was now doing standing quads. *Perky heffa.* "You got this."

Glaring at my big sister, I grumbled, "First the fuck of all, I know I got this. Second, I haven't run in a week. I needed a slow start, a jog. Not a damn sprint."

That slide into home had been worse for my body than I could've imagined. The next day, I could hardly move. My mother had brought me food and helped me clean up. It'd taken all week for me to even walk straight. Long gone were the days I could bounce back and keep it moving. And apparently, the days when I could drink all night and get up at the butt crack of dawn to run were a distant memory too.

Bliss, who'd run ahead of us minutes ago, circled back around. Another one who acted like she could do this all day. Looking at her, I'd never know she'd given birth less than six months ago. "Why'd you stop? We have pedicure appointments in a couple of hours, and I'd like to eat breakfast." And she ate more than all of us too.

"What the hell is going on here?" Blake circled back around. "I was just talking about something important when I noticed I was alone." She pushed Paityn. "You could've told me to stop running."

Pointing at me, Paityn shrugged. "She's tired. I stopped with her."

"Already?" Blake glanced at her watch. "I can't with you, Dallas. We haven't even hit a mile. I need more steps. Duke and I are in a competition."

"Well then, take your ass on." I gestured for her to keep

it moving. "Don't let me stop you." I sat down on a park bench. Needless to say, I wasn't finishing this run. I'd already decided to walk to the smoothie place around the corner and get my favorite drink. "I can just meet y'all later."

Bliss hugged me, catching me so off guard that I almost fell over. When she pulled back, she gave me a cheeky grin and a shrug. "Sorry to spring that on you. But you look like you need a hug."

Even on my worst days, a hug from Bliss was always a good thing. "Thanks, Sissy," I said.

"Any time. We should eat ice cream for breakfast." We called her our own personal cheering section, because she rooted hard for everybody "Young." Bliss was the heart of our family. Loving and genuinely kind, giving and positive. I loved the hell out of her.

Tyn sat next to me. "You two go on. I'll stay with Dallas."

"Sure?" Blake asked.

Paityn nodded. "We'll meet you back at the house."

Blake and Bliss took off, leaving me alone with Paityn.

"Are you really okay, Dallas?"

While Bliss was the heart, Paityn was the nurturer. She'd always considered herself Momma 2.0. And all of us agreed, even Tristan. Whenever we needed something, whether it was a place to hide or a peach cobbler, she had us covered. A couple of years ago, she'd made the decision to put herself and her dreams first and had moved to California. After a few short weeks on the west coast, she'd met the love of her life. I'd never seen her happier, but I missed her terribly.

"I'm good," I told her. "A lot on my mind."

"Thinking about the brewing scandal?"

I snorted. "That shit is already brewed *and* poured." Maya had set up a brunch for tomorrow so I could meet the Color of Law board members. It'd been a long time since I'd been nervous about anything, but I had teetered between making up an excuse to not attend and just telling her I wasn't interested. "What if I'm not doing the right thing?"

She eyed me out of the corner of her eye. "You don't even sound like yourself."

"I know! I sound like a lil' bitch."

Paityn cracked up. "You sound like your ten-year-old self."

"I don't miss that kid." At ten, I'd struggled to find my place in the family. Everyone seemed to have a pair. Paityn and Tristan were tight because they were the oldest. Duke and Dex were the twins, while I was the odd girl out. Blake and Bliss had each other and *their* twin thing. And Asa was the baby. I remembered feeling so alone in a house full of people. It wasn't until I met Demi that things started to change for me. She became *my* pair.

"*I* do," Paityn admitted.

I frowned. "What?"

"That kid needed me. She wasn't afraid to show vulnerability, she wasn't always trying to be strong, and she wasn't fixing everyone's life."

I swallowed as tears filled my eyes. "Paityn, if you make me cry, I'm going to push you off this damn bench."

She wrapped her arms around me and pulled me into a tight embrace. "I'll stop. I love you, Sissy. I just want you to be okay."

I leaned my forehead against her shoulder. "Why wouldn't I be okay?"

"Because you're so busy being Dallas Young, Marriage

Broker, Badass Boss Bitch. Don't get me wrong, I'm so proud of you. You are killin' it out here. But I just wonder if you're really happy."

Pulling back, I nodded. "I am. My family makes me happy. My career makes me happy."

"So why do you look so sad to me?"

My mouth fell open. I didn't have words; I didn't have an argument. And I *always* had an argument.

Paityn raised a challenging brow. "I get it, you love your job. But remember when Blake was too afraid to admit she was in love with Lennox? You were the main one encouraging her to do it. When I was going back and forth with my feelings for Bishop, you were right there telling me to get my shit together."

"That's different," I argued. "In both cases, there was an existing relationship y'all were trying to fuck up. By the way, I'm not a novice at this psych shit. You keep trying to sneak in a therapy session, and I don't like it. Between Bliss sending me matches and Mom introducing me to 'nice' young men, I'm over it. Please don't become that older sister trying to marry her single sisters off. I thought you were better than that, Tyn."

"That's not what I was doing. And I'm not that much older."

"Sounds like it to me. Right now, I'm focused on my career and I'm okay with that."

"But what happens when you hit that goal?"

"There's always another one," I replied.

"What about after work?"

"Oh God, you sound like Mom."

"I am her daughter." Paityn bumped my shoulder with hers. "Okay, I'll stop. I just want you happy and fulfilled."

I blew out a slow breath. "*If* I decide to let someone

into my heart, it'll be when *I* want to do it. Until then, I'm good. I don't need a man to feel fulfilled."

"I never said you did. That's not what this is about. I just haven't seen you happy in years, not since…"

A pang of guilt nearly took my breath away. I groaned, unwilling to go any further with this conversation. I had stuff to do. "Girl! You're a sex therapist. Stop trying to be my shrink."

Paityn burst out laughing. "You're silly for that."

"Oh, I'm so serious. If you're going to offer me therapy, how about you invent another B.A.D. so I can try that shit out." My sister had successfully launched a naughty toy line. Her products were appealing to a growing number of young black men and women. I especially loved the dildo, Big Ass D, or B.A.D.

"It's coming," she offered. "You'll be the first to get the prototype."

"Thanks. Now, can we go get my smoothie? I'm thirsty."

"Fine." Paityn stood and pulled me to my feet. "I'm done playing Momma 2.0."

"Good."

It didn't take us long to walk home after we stopped at the smoothie café. When we arrived, I noticed Maya's car in the driveway.

"Is that Maya?" Paityn asked.

I nodded and knocked on the window. Maya jumped and motioned to her phone. Once she ended her call, she got out of the car. "Hi." Paityn and Maya exchanged hugs. "So good to see you."

"I know," Tyn said. "It's been a while."

"We'll have to catch up soon." Maya glanced my way. "Have you seen this?" She held up her phone. I squinted my eyes and read the headline: WHO IS DALLAS DOING NOW?

My eyes widened when I saw the photograph. It was taken outside of my house, earlier in the week. With Preston.

Paityn leaned in, reading the small screen. "Oh, shit."

My sister hated the word "shit." Which meant this really was an *Oh, Shit* moment if she said it. "Exactly," I murmured.

Paityn gasped. "Is that Preston?"

I shot Tyn a sidelong glare. "Yes." I peered at Maya. "I don't know what to say."

"Is this your boyfriend?" Maya asked.

Shaking my head rapidly, I repeated the word no about five times before I added, "Not at all. He's just a friend." *I'm such a freakin' liar.* That last interaction with him had proven there was more than simple friendship at play. One false move, and we would've been fucking again. Scuffed knee, bad hip, and all.

"*Can* he be your man?"

"What?" The question was asked simultaneously—by me and Tyn.

"Look, I hate to do this. But this might not be a bad thing." Maya held up her hand. "Hear me out. What if we go with it? He's your friend. Would he mind coming to some events, playing the role? Just until this publicity blows over."

"Why would I do that?" I asked. "Maya, I think it's probably best you find someone else. I'm not about that fake-romance life. And I'm not a liar."

"It could work, though," Paityn mused. "Besides, you wouldn't be lying. There are sparks between you and Preston."

"Shut up," I grumbled.

Maya shrugged. "If there are sparks, then this might be beneficial in other ways."

"No."

"Just…think about it." Maya squeezed my shoulders. "In the meantime, go into this brunch tomorrow ready to wow them."

Maya stayed and chatted with me and Paityn for a few minutes before she left.

Back in the house, Paityn gave Blake and Bliss the rundown.

"Actually, I think it's a good idea," Bliss said. "I've always liked Preston. He's amazing."

"And fine as hell," Blake added.

"I don't care," I shouted. "I'm not going to pretend to date him." After spending time with Preston, I was certain he was dealing with something bigger than this. Even if it was a good idea, I didn't want to add a farce onto his already full plate. "Besides, he… Never mind. I'm not doing it. If it isn't in the cards for me to become a full member of this organization, so be it."

"Is this something you want?" Paityn asked.

I pinned her with a glare. "Are we starting this again?"

"No." She raised her hands in surrender. "Just a question."

"Even if I didn't want it, I'll be damned if Kimball Payne and his phony-ass wife keep me from doing anything."

"Sissy, answer the damn question," Bliss pressed. "We have an appointment."

I sat on the arm of my couch and sipped my water. Sighing, I nodded. "I do want this, but…"

"But…?" Blake motioned for me to continue.

Admittedly, I was torn. Between what I wanted and what I needed. I didn't *need* the hassle of a PR campaign just to prove I was worthy. And I wouldn't lie to make myself look better. "Never mind." I went to my room without another word. There was no sense in talking about this. I'd already accomplished so much, and I knew I'd get where I wanted to be eventually—even without the Color of Law Organization.

Chapter Six

MAKE IT RAIN

Preston

"Nephew!"

I bent to give my Aunt Dot a kiss to her brow. "Hey, Auntie."

I'd reached out to Aunt Dot when my mother had failed to return home, just to check in and see if she'd heard from her. While the two sisters were estranged, Dot knew all the people in their old neighborhood and all my mother's hangouts. So, she'd quickly tracked Mom down.

For the past week, I'd received several texts from my aunt, updating me on my mother's whereabouts. A couple of days ago, Aunt Dot had called to let me know Mom had finally made her way back home.

Aunt Dot placed her palm over mine and smiled. "It's so good to see you, son. You look handsome as ever." My aunt was ten years older than Mom, and they couldn't be more different. Aunt Dot was married to a pastor and was a pillar in her community. She'd raised money for charities, conducted an annual coat drive for young kids, and spearheaded the church missionary department. She'd traveled all over, visiting multiple countries to provide aid to disadvantaged adults and youth. And she didn't drink, not even a wine cooler.

I flipped my palm over and held her hand. "And you look beautiful as always, Auntie."

Growing up, Aunt Dot had offered me a safe place, somewhere to go when I'd needed a break from my mother. Aunt Dot had even opened up her home multiple times for me to live with her. Luckily, she'd lived on the next block so I'd had easy access to her house. When the situation called for it, she'd come get me and wait for my mother to go into treatment. My mother would inevitably do just that but would always fall off the wagon. Always. It was a vicious cycle, one that had taken a toll on me. As soon as I'd been old enough to have a say, though, I'd decided to stay in the house with Mom, because I felt someone had to be there. Even after I'd done that, my aunt made sure she helped me as much as possible, which I appreciated.

"How is she?" I asked after the waitress took our drink order.

Once a month, I treated my aunt to brunch at The Gandy Dancer in Ann Arbor. It was my way of thanking her for everything she'd done for me. Because, real talk, if she hadn't been there, I wouldn't be here.

My aunt let out a heavy sigh. "According to Rod Pierce, she hasn't left the house since she returned. He's seen some delivery cars out front, but that's it. What happened?"

Telling my aunt about my mother's revelation wasn't something I wanted to do over the phone. Every time she'd asked me any questions about what had transpired between me and my mom, I'd told her I'd fill her in at brunch. "I went to see her last weekend," I explained. "She was…" I shook my head, trying to shake the image of the house out of my mind. "She was hungover, disheveled. She hadn't cleaned—the house or herself."

"Jesus," Aunt Dot whispered. "Oh, Heavenly Father, help her."

I smiled. My aunt was known to break out in prayer or praise at any moment. Whenever I needed to get a prayer through, I called her. "She was behind on her bills," I continued. "I agreed to pay them. She was already agitated, so when I asked her some questions, she went off and accused me of being like my father."

Aunt Dot frowned. "That's not a bad thing. Your father was a good man."

Whenever I thought about the man I'd thought was my father, I felt two things at once. I missed him, because he'd died when I was too young to get to know him as a man. And I resented him, because he'd left me to suffer with my mother. Today, that feeling of resentment was strong. "Interesting," I mused.

"What?" she asked. "I know you and your father had a strained relationship, but he loved you."

I rubbed the back of my neck. "I know, Auntie."

"So, what's the problem?"

The waitress returned with coffee and orange juice. She explained the buffet process and shared the chef's featured entree.

Grinning, my aunt rubbed her hands together. "Ooh, sounds delicious. Although, I think I'll have the eggs benedict today."

When the waitress walked away, I stood and pulled out my aunt's chair. We made our way over to the buffet. As we piled our plates, my mind stayed on the conversation ahead. Of course, I'd done my own research, searching my mother's business documents, looking at her high school yearbooks, old pictures my late grandmother had given me. I found nothing, not even a small clue. My birth certificate listed Preston Hayes Sr. as my father.

My aunt happily hummed a church devotional as she scooped fresh fruit onto her plate, while I asked the carver to slice me a piece of roast beef. It almost felt like there was too much food available today. There were so many good options, it was hard to choose what to eat. In the end, I decided on a fresh Belgian waffle and hash browns instead of the made-to-order omelet.

I stepped over to the waffle station and made my request. There was someone in line ahead of me, so I knew I'd have to wait a bit. I picked a blueberry off my plate and popped it in my mouth.

"Don't look now, but someone is watching you."

I smiled to myself, immediately recognizing the voice. I glanced over. "Hey, Dallas."

She leaned closer. "You're literally turning heads in this restaurant. Like the woman over there by the cheese blintzes. She can barely concentrate on her plate because she's so busy watching you."

Chuckling, I whispered, "Is she cute?"

She tapped her chin. "Beautiful. And my mother's age. If you're into the cougar thing. She might buy you a car."

I barked out a laugh. "My lease is up in a few months. It would be good timing."

Dallas pointed at me. "Don't play now. They are some freaks. One of the ladies in my group keeps talking about her latest erotic romance read. No shame. She was checking you out too. Said you were fine, like one of the strong black heroes in her books."

I smirked. "Did you agree with her?"

Dallas rolled her eyes. "Boy, shut up." She requested a waffle. "What brings you here on this Sunday morning?"

"I'm treating my aunt to brunch."

"That's nice. Good nephew."

The chef placed my hot waffle on my plate. "Why are you here?" I asked her.

"I'm meeting with ladies from Color of Law. They're evaluating my worthiness for full membership in their organization."

"Ah, okay."

"In reality, I don't even know what I'm doing here. So much going on, and I don't particularly want a bunch of women judging me or questioning my choices. You know?"

"Well, you can always leave. Spend your Sunday with your family."

She sighed. "No, I'm not going to do that. I want this too bad."

"What's going on?"

Dallas bit down on her bottom lip. "That's right, you probably don't read the blogs or watch YouTube videos."

"No. Am I missing something?"

"Yeah, kind of."

An older woman walked over to us. "Dallas, is everything okay?" The lady smiled at me and held out her hand. "Hello, I'm Maya. And you're Preston Hayes."

Confused by this turn of events and curious how Maya knew who I was, I glanced at Dallas. Only, she didn't look at me because she was laser focused on her plate. I shook Maya's hand. "I am. I'm sorry, I don't remember meeting you."

"Oh, we haven't met. But I've seen you."

"Preston?" my aunt called. "I'm heading back to the table."

"You'd better go," Dallas said. "We'll talk?"

Something was going on, but I would wait until I could talk to Dallas in private. I nodded. "Call me." I said my goodbyes and went back to our table.

When I sat down, my aunt smirked. "Who was that beautiful young woman?"

I glanced back at the buffet, meeting Dallas' gaze briefly before she disappeared. "She's a friend."

"A friend who obviously has her eye on you."

I smiled. "How do you figure?"

"I've been married for over forty years, nephew. I know when a woman is interested in a man."

"I don't know about that." Yet, even as I said the words, I couldn't help but wonder if Aunt Dot was on to something.

We ate in silence for a few minutes before my aunt brought us back to the subject at hand. "Are you going to talk to me?" I eyed her over the rim of my glass. "You've always been so closed off, quiet. I worry about you."

"I'm fine," I assured.

"It's in your eyes. You do a great job of hiding it, but I saw it then. And I see it now. You're not fine. Tell me what's wrong."

I set my glass down. "Mom told me something the last time I saw her, and I can't wrap my brain around it. It doesn't make sense to me."

"Your mom says a lot of things that don't make sense. It's the liquor."

"Aunt Dot, I don't think it was the liquor this time. I think she was angry, and she wanted to hurt me."

She put her fork down. "Oh, boy. Lord, help us." She blew out a slow breath, then said, "Okay, hit me with it."

"Before she closed herself in the bathroom, she told me my father wasn't my father."

Aunt Dot's eyes widened, but she didn't look shocked. "Wow."

"You knew?" I asked.

Her gaze darted around the room. "I…I had suspicions. Your mother loved Hayes, but she wasn't faithful to him."

"Why am I just now finding this out?" My body tensed as anger welled up inside me. I expected my mother to lie, but I'd never thought Aunt Dot would know something this important and not say anything. "Why wouldn't you tell me?"

"Son, please. I didn't know anything for sure. All I know is there were rumors. Rumors are not facts."

"And you never thought I should know? I've been walking around here oblivious." I was ready to explode. I counted to ten, hoping it would calm me down a little bit. The last thing I wanted to do was disrespect the only woman who'd shown me maternal-like love. "I just don't understand why you wouldn't tell me. Even if it was a rumor."

Aunt Dot rocked back and forth, muttering prayers under her breath. "This is a mess. God doesn't like mess."

"I understand that, but don't you think I should know who my father is?"

A tear fell from her eye. "Before your mother got pregnant, she was hanging around with a man who wasn't from here. He lived on the other side of the state, but he would often come to Detroit, flashing his money around. Women would throw themselves at him. Your mother caught his eye. She was beautiful back then. I heard they had a short-lived affair."

"He was married?"

She nodded. "It didn't last long. He disappeared, and I never heard anything about him again. A couple of months later, she was engaged to your father. Then, you came."

"Who is he? I want to reach out to him."

My aunt squeezed her napkin. "You can't."

"Why?"

"He's dead."

My shoulders fell. Any hope of finding answers evaporated with those two words. *He's dead.* There would be no resolution, no confirmations, no talks with the man who could've been my father. Still, I needed to know more. "What's his name?"

My aunt swallowed visibly. "Parker Wells Sr."

LATER, I was neck-deep in information. I'd spent the rest of the afternoon researching Parker Wells Sr. Every article, every news clip. It was impossible to be a resident of Michigan and not know who the man was. Wellspring Water Corporation was one of the biggest water companies in the state. Shit, the country.

There was just one problem. From all accounts, he was a monster. In every aspect. According to one article, if he'd lived, he would've probably been prosecuted for various crimes, including conspiracy and corporate fraud. Another write-up mentioned it was his daughter who'd discovered his transgressions and had turned him in.

Mr. Wells' shady business dealings were just the tip of the iceberg. His first wife had died under mysterious circumstances, then he'd gone on to marry multiple women. He was also well known for his indiscretions, and two of his four kids had been born to mistresses. *And I might be his third.*

When the man had died, his son, Parker Wells Jr., took over the company, and the estate had been split between his known kids. I'd just clicked on an article about his youngest son, who was now the Assistant City Planner for Wellspring, Michigan, when I heard a knock at the door.

The brunch with my aunt hadn't ended so much as I'd left her sitting there alone. In hindsight, I realized how fucked up that was, but I needed to get away. It'd be just like Aunt Dot to give me a few hours before stopping by to check on me.

I closed my laptop and walked over to the door. When I peeked through the small window, I had to do a double take. Because it definitely wasn't my aunt. I opened the door. "Hey."

Dallas flashed a quick smile. "Sorry to just pop up on you. But can we talk?" I held the door open wider, allowing her to enter. She brushed past me. "Thanks for not slamming the door in my face."

"Never." I gestured toward my leather sofa. "Have a seat."

Only she didn't sit. She walked around the room, presumably checking my place out. Then, it dawned on me that she'd never been inside before. I wasn't a person who had parties or game nights or anything else for that matter. So, there was never a reason for her to come to my house.

"Did you want something to drink?" I asked.

She shook her head. "No, thanks. You have a nice home. I love the grays. Always so Zen."

I leaned against the kitchen island. "Thanks."

"Listen, I won't take up too much of your time, but I wanted to talk to you about today at the restaurant."

The little interaction with Dallas today had felt like a reprieve, the light part of my dark day. Even though it had been weird. "Yeah, what was that about?"

"So, Maya is on the board of Color of Law. She

approached me about possibly running for office in the near future."

Impressed, I folded my arms over my chest. "Really? That's pretty amazing." I had no doubt Dallas had the knowledge and charisma to win any race she ran.

"It's a big deal."

"You were meeting with that group to discuss their plans for you?"

She nodded. "And so they could meet me."

"How did it go?"

She paused for a moment before she said, "Good."

"Okay."

"Here's the thing…as you know, I've had some issues with the blogs and such."

Dallas had briefly mentioned the issues she'd been having since a pic of her with Kimball Payne had surfaced online. "Right. You shared that you received a wedding invitation."

Her soft giggle felt forced, like she was trying to find the humor in everything going on. "Exactly. I'm apparently marrying my ho-ish ways."

I hated the connotation. I'd had to fight my way through middle and high school because guys—and sometimes girls—had liked to call my mother a ho. I didn't think it was funny at all. "That was bullshit."

"It's stupid," she agreed.

"Dallas, what—"

"There was another article," she interrupted, pulling her phone out of her purse. She stepped forward, holding it up for me to see.

I took it from her and scanned the headline, pausing at the picture for a moment before reading the article. When I finished, I met her gaze. "This is us." Everything started to click, to fall into place. "That's how your mentor knew who I was."

"Exactly."

"They think we're together?"

"Or they think you're just another notch on my proverbial belt."

My mind raced with potential drawbacks to this type of publicity. And knowing that she wanted a political future… "How does this affect you?"

She shrugged. "Maya thinks it might help if I had a 'beard' of sorts. Someone to go to events with, to…" She threw her hands up in the air. "Hell, I don't know. Pretend. Just until the media finds someone else to focus on."

Considering everything that had happened in my world over the past two weeks, the thought of distracting myself with Dallas was very appealing. And since I didn't beat around the bush, I asked, "What if I help you?"

She met my gaze full on. "It's funny you said that. Maya thinks it's a good idea if you did."

So that's why Maya was looking at me like she knew something I didn't know. And why Dallas *wasn't* looking at me. "And what do you think?" I handed her the phone. "Is that what you want?"

Dallas searched my face. "I don't want to lie. That's not who I am."

"How about we reframe it then?" I suggested. "We're friends. My friend needs an assist. And I'm happy to help."

"I can't ask you to do this."

"You didn't."

She bit down on her bottom lip. "Preston, this is crazy. I'm not even sure it's worth it."

I brushed a strand of hair out of her face, enjoying that her eyes fluttered closed. "Do you want this?"

"I do," she admitted. "But not at the expense of my integrity."

"So we just don't say what we are. That way, you're not lying. We let people assume that we're together. And you know what they say about assumptions, right?"

She smirked. "Right."

"Okay, then. I'll show up when you need me to."

"If we do this, I want to keep it professional. I know we're friends, but it helps me to think of this as an arrangement. You're doing me a favor, and I'm grateful. But I—"

"Dallas, tell me what you need. You're the negotiator, correct? Let's negotiate." My gaze dropped to her mouth. *So ready to be kissed.*

"Now you're talking my language." She pulled out her phone and typed something on the screen. "I think it's important we set our expectations early so there's no confusion. First, we don't have to make any statements to reporters. And we don't necessarily have to have public displays of affection."

I smirked. "When exactly can we display it?" Her eyes flashed to mine, and I added, "I just want to make sure I'm playing my role correctly. You know I'm a perfectionist."

"No PDA, Preston," she repeated.

"What about private?" I asked. She hid it well, but I'd caught the soft hitch in her breath, the way she swayed on her feet. And the only thing I could think of was, *This is going to be fun.*

Dallas ignored my question. "We can come up with a concrete plan tomorrow?"

"Dinner?"

"In public," she countered.

"If we're going to talk, it should probably be where no one can hear our conversation."

She cursed. "Public dinner, private talk."

I held out a hand, and she slipped hers into mine. "Deal."

With her eyes locked on mine, she nodded. "Deal." After a moment, she cleared her throat. "Preston?"

"Yes?"

"You're touching me. My hand."

I hadn't realized I was still holding it. I let go. "Sorry."

She averted her gaze. "Alright. I'll call you and we can discuss the place and time."

"Got it."

"Thanks, Preston." She blessed me with another smile, then she left.

I wanted to walk her out to her car, but I sensed she'd rather I not. I would give her that—this time. But something told me we'd just made a deal that would change everything for us. And I was here for it.

Chapter Seven

SOMEONE TO WATCH OVER ME

Dallas

With every passing day, I found myself feeling extremely uncomfortable in my surroundings. Going to the grocery store felt like an exercise in futility, because I couldn't even pick a decent cucumber without eyes on me, without whispers about me from random women on the street, without someone making a comment about Kimball Payne and his trifling wife, Yasmin Ray. I was good at ignoring shit, but it'd become increasingly hard to tune out the noise.

Ordinary routines were now complicated. Instead of taking Washtenaw Avenue, I'd used the side streets on my ride home, a different route every day. To avoid being photographed outside my house, I'd hired a lawn service to cut my grass and do the things around my house I'd always loved to do.

Every public outing had turned into a huge deal. Like

now, I was sitting in the middle of one of the best seafood restaurants in Ann Arbor and my mind was on everything but the Paella Valenciana in front of me. I stared down at the dish, one of my favorites. The smell of chicken, chorizo sausage, and spices made me hungry. But I couldn't eat.

I felt a soft elbow against my side. I peered over at Maya, who was watching me with concerned eyes. "Are you okay, sweetie?"

I pushed my fork around my plate and nodded. "I'm fine." I forced a smile on my face, even knowing she'd never believe it was real.

"Thanks for coming on such short notice," she said.

"It's no trouble." When Maya had called that morning, I'd been finalizing plans to meet Preston for dinner tonight—to discuss our deal. The week had been so hectic that we hadn't had the chance to finish our discussion from Sunday. As a result, I'd started to feel anxious about pretending to be with someone for professional gain. Preston must've sensed I needed to talk about this, because he'd offered to meet me here after dinner for a dessert.

Somehow that made it worse. He seemed to know what I needed without me asking. This wasn't a recent development either. Even on my birthday, he'd understood what I wanted and had given it to me. No expectations, no promises. *One night. One fuck.* I would've never asked him to lie for me, despite how great of an idea my sisters and Maya thought it was. He probably knew that too. I suspected that was why he'd initiated it, why he'd made the offer. And I could do nothing but accept his help. His lips, his body, his voice, his eyes… He'd already visited me in my dreams too many times to count. Close proximity would definitely be a challenge.

"You seem distracted," Maya said, pulling me from my thoughts. "Are you sure you're okay, Dallas?"

I shrugged. "Just tired." That part was the truth. I was exhausted from having to suck it up and keep it moving. I was drained from the constant speculation about me. And I was worn out from always having to be "on." The more time passed, the more I wanted to quit. I hadn't been myself in weeks, and no matter what I'd done to push through, I couldn't stop obsessing about all the drama.

Maya leaned closer, whispering under her breath, "Let me know if this is too much. I don't like seeing you like this."

I offered her another smile—this time a real one. It felt good to know she had my back regardless. "I'll reevaluate after the weekend."

Maya nodded, turning her attention to her lobster tail. I speared a piece of sausage with my fork, intent on finally putting food in my stomach.

A board member cleared her throat. "Ms. Young, I wanted to have dinner with you tonight to discuss a few concerns that several of our members have."

Here we go.

"A new, bright light has shined on your personal life. In light of this development, do you feel you can be an effective member of our organization?"

Maya interjected, "Susan, as I've explained many times, I was there when Ms. Young saw Kimball Payne. He approached her, and she walked away. Nothing improper happened. Last I checked, it wasn't a crime to talk to someone on the street."

"But you understand that we value discretion, Maya. In times like these, we cannot afford to let our guard down or become embroiled in scandal. You of all people should know the toll bad publicity takes."

Maya set her glass down. "I also know it's never a good idea to concern ourselves with what happens behind closed doors between consenting adults." Maya's divorce had been bitter and very public. Her ex-husband had waged a campaign against her because she'd left him for another woman. In the end, everything had worked out, but it had been a precarious time of motion after motion, court dates, mediation, and multiple settlement conferences.

"Whether the rumors are true or not, public perception says they are," Susan said.

"May I speak?" I asked.

Susan gestured for me to continue. "By all means."

"I understand your concerns. However, current rumors aside, when is it ever acceptable to punish first and ask questions later? We're all attorneys. We should know the concept of due process, of believing that every person is innocent until proven guilty."

"Yes, that's true," Susan conceded. "Still, we're trying to build something. I would like to think people vote the issues, the policies, as opposed to the person. Unfortunately, that isn't the case."

"It's not just the drama with Kimball," another woman added. "The narrative is already spun. Not only are you being portrayed as a home wrecker, but the latest is that you're…loose."

I squeezed my fork hard. My heart pounded in my ear as heat flushed through my body. It had already been a tense night. I didn't want to get into this here, but the idea that I was a ho because I dated different men pissed me the fuck off. Still, I held my head high when I said, "I believe every woman has the right to decide what she does with her own body. Even if I was, as you say, loose, it would be no one's business but mine."

Maya coughed. "Listen, this is counterproductive. We

say we fight for the rights of women in this field, of all women. Why would we turn our backs on a qualified, talented attorney for baseless lies? Susan, when your husband cheated on you with his student, who had your back? We did. Anna, when you drank too much and crashed your car into someone's house, who showed up? Me. I believe we owe it to Dallas to consider her based on her work in the community. Not this bullshit."

In that moment, I didn't know where to look. Maya's clapback had effectively shut everyone at the table up. And the fact that she'd added in that well-placed *bullshit* made me want to stand up and clap.

Time stretched on with no other comments from the board members. Eventually, Susan sighed. "I think we should all take a step back. Let's table this discussion for another day."

Everyone except Maya agreed. Then, she mouthed, *I'm sorry*.

Just as I was about to excuse myself to go to the restroom, another woman approached the table. "Dallas Young?"

"Yes?" The woman was around my mother's age, or maybe a little older. Several of the women at the table greeted her warmly, as if they'd known her for ages. But I couldn't place where I'd seen her before. Her downturned mouth and her hard glare told me she didn't like me, though. My immediate thought was she was somehow connected to this Kimball mess, but she could've just as easily encountered me another way. During my years practicing divorce law and now concentrating on settlement agreements between future spouses, I'd made some enemies. "How can I help you?"

"You've done enough actually," the woman sneered, flashing a cold smile.

"I'm sorry, but I don't know what you're referring to. Obviously, you know me from somewhere. Care to refresh my memory?" I took a second to assess the ladies at the table, who were watching the scene intently, no doubt wondering how I'd respond.

"You represented Langton Sykes in a prenuptial agreement?"

I froze, realization dawning on me. The woman standing here, glaring at me, was the mother of Langston's future bride. Mrs. Irene Turner. "Yes, I did," I confirmed.

She looked me up and down, her disdain for me clear. "Langston told us how you behaved, the way you propositioned him and threatened to destroy his relationship with my daughter if he didn't do what you wanted."

"Wait a minute," Maya interjected. "Who—"

I placed a hand on her's and squeezed, effectively letting her know I didn't need her to defend me.

"I guess I shouldn't be surprised you behaved the way you did," the woman continued. "I've read that you enjoy wrecking homes. I'm just glad he fired you. My daughter doesn't need that negative energy going into her marriage."

"Thank you for your candor, Mrs. Turner," I said. "Allow me the same?"

She stiffened. "That's not necessary."

"Oh, but it is. For the record, Langston fed you and your daughter a bunch of lies." *Bullshit* was a better word, and would've hit better, but we were in a very public restaurant. The last thing I needed was another headline detailing my potty mouth. "Just as he's portrayed himself to be a standup man. Let's be clear—in the interest of helping *your* daughter, *I* fired *him*. Meaning, I told him to find another attorney. The notion that I'd ruin my professional reputation by hitting on a client is ludicrous. The idea that I'd risk my license for Langston Sykes is laughable. Really."

"Why would he lie, Ms. Young?" Mrs. Turner asked.

"Why wouldn't he?" I countered. "Our one and only meeting ended when I asked him to leave my office. Langston demonstrated he doesn't respect *any* woman by insisting on adding unreasonable and archaic provisions in the prenuptial agreement. By the way, *any* woman includes *your* daughter."

"Don't talk about my daughter. I will ruin you."

"Bring it," I said. "I don't regret how I handled the situation. There was no impropriety on my behalf. Simply put, my commitment to the edification of women—of *black* women—would not allow me to continue serving as his counsel. Therefore, I released him and returned his retainer. How that translated to me throwing myself at him, I don't know. But maybe it's something you need to get to the bottom of before your daughter walks down that aisle to forever. Or until she gives him a reason to enforce one of the provisions he'd been too keen on including in their prenuptial agreement. Now, if you'll excuse me…" I dropped my napkin to the table and stood. Yet, instead of making my bad-ass exit, I turned into a very hard chest.

Strong arms wrapped around my waist, holding me steady. "Sorry."

I peered up, into the eyes of my *man*. "Preston?" I breathed.

"Run with it," he murmured against my ear, right before he brushed his lips over my temple, then my cheek. "You did good. I'll take it from here." Before I could object, he kissed me. Well, it wasn't a kiss so much as it was a soft touch of his mouth to mine. But it felt like he'd pulled me close, like he'd used his mouth, his teeth, and his tongue.

"Oh," I whispered, unable to form any other words. I stared at his lips.

He looked over my head and smiled. "Hello, I'm Preston," he said, stepping away from me to greet the older women.

Snapping out of the trance he'd put me in, I glanced down at Maya, who was grinning ear to ear. I watched him charm the other women at the table. While he was schmoozing, I raked my gaze over his tall frame. There was something about a man who knew how to wear his clothes. His navy pants and white shirt could easily segue from the office to the bar. His silver watch glinted in the dim light, drawing my attention to his arms. *Lord.* He had great arms —strong, defined muscles. Obviously, he spent a lot of time in the gym. But I also knew he didn't mind doing manual labor and would often work onsite with his crew, nailing boards, hauling wood, carrying steel beams, or some shit like that. Either way, I appreciated his form, the way he moved. And the way Susan fluttered her eyelashes like a damn teenager when he'd complimented her let me know she did too.

After several more dimpled smiles and low chuckles, Preston turned his attention to Mrs. Turner. He didn't introduce himself to her, though. Instead, he said, "Don't let us keep you from your party."

Mrs. Turner gaped. "Excuse me?"

Preston pointed toward the front of the restaurant, where a small group of people were watching the scene unfold. "I overheard them mentioning they were ready to go. Something about an art exhibit?"

She blinked.

"If you're going to the Van Gogh Immersive Art exhibit, you should probably get there a little early. The lines are long."

Mrs. Turner's fair skin turned bright red, and she opened her mouth to speak, but nothing came out. Instead, she glared at me then walked away without another word.

Preston winked at me and proceeded to trace small circles over my hip. He smelled like wood, leather, and oranges. *Delicious*. Between his fingers working their magic on me and his scent, I struggled to maintain my composure. I had no idea what they were even talking about at this point, because I was laser focused on him.

I registered Maya's laugh, which pulled me from my totally inappropriate thoughts about Preston's dick. "Exactly," my mentor said, laughing in delight.

I briefly wondered what I'd missed, and my need for self-preservation made me maneuver out of his grasp. But then, Preston pulled me back to him, pressing his warm lips against my forehead.

"I hope I didn't interrupt something important," he said. "We thought a little dessert after dinner would be nice. Date night."

Susan's face lit up. "Sounds lovely, Mr. Hayes."

"Call me Preston," he told her.

"Aren't you the young man in the latest photo with our Dallas?" Susan asked.

Our Dallas?

"Yes, ma'am," Preston told her, smoothing his hand over my back.

If he didn't stop touching me… *Business. Professional.*

"Are you and Dallas together?" Anna asked.

Preston chuckled, meeting my gaze. His eyes blazed with something I wasn't sure I wanted to name, something sincere, something real. "We are." His expression softened. "It was a long time coming, but I'm grateful she chose me. I'm a very lucky man."

Dammit, even I believed him. *Business. This is not a thing.*

"Well, don't let us keep you from your date," Maya said. "I got dinner, Dallas. I'll call you later."

"Are you sure?" I asked. Now, Preston was brushing the back of my neck with his talented fingers. And I was trying to convince myself this was just a business arrangement, no matter how good his hands felt against my skin. It wasn't working. *Shit.*

Maya squeezed my hand and stood, embracing me and giving me a small reprieve from Preston's hands—and his cologne. "Love it," she whispered. "I'll call you later."

I said my goodbyes to the women and let Preston lead me to a quiet booth in the corner of the restaurant. He remained standing while I slid into the booth. And when he sat next to me, I nearly slipped under the table, trying to put some space between us. "What are you doing?" I asked through clenched teeth.

"Acting like your man," he said with a shrug.

"Can they even see us?"

He leaned over and waved at them. "Yep," he mumbled. "And they're watching."

I couldn't see them, but I believed him. "Fine. What happened to letting people assume we're together but not actually telling anyone we're a couple?"

"I had to improvise. Did you really want dessert?"

"And I thought I said no PDA?"

He picked up the menu. "How about key lime pie?"

"Preston? We agreed that—"

With his eyes still on the menu, he muttered, "Like I said, I had to improvise." Then, he pinned me with his intense stare. "Can we negotiate improvisation, counselor?"

Swallowing hard, I relented. "Sure. But can you not do that again?"

"Do what?" he asked. "I think I remember you telling me you loved crème brûlée?"

"I don't…" *Want your dessert* died on my lips when I realized what he'd just said. "You remembered that?"

A corner of his mouth lifted. "I remember everything."

A smile tugged at my lips. I remembered that night too. He and Cooper had met me and Blake at my favorite Italian restaurant. I'd been craving dessert and couldn't wait to order it. But the waitress had kindly doused my flames when she'd told us they weren't preparing it that evening for whatever reason. Talk about devastated. I almost couldn't eat my meal because I was so disappointed. *Almost.*

"You were irritated," he continued. "I also remember you'd just run your first 4k and had trained for weeks with no dessert."

Damn, he's good. And extremely sexy.

"It was your treat to yourself for finishing in the top twenty." He lifted his hand and brushed his thumb over my chin.

I held my breath. "Preston." I tried to keep my voice strong, even. But it sounded breathy and affected.

He traced my jaw line with his finger and cupped my cheek with his massive palm. "Dallas."

"You're touching me," I murmured.

"So?"

"No PDA," I said lamely. "A kiss is public and affection."

He leaned in, so close I could smell the hint of mint on his breath. "Nah. *That* wasn't PDA," he whispered before pressing his lips to mine. The kiss was soft, just like the one earlier. Tender. Still, it seared me, branded me in a way. I tried to fight the pull, tried to talk myself out of this, but I couldn't bring myself to stop. "*This* is PDA," he whispered, opening his mouth and sucking on my bottom lip until I groaned.

Now, this kiss… *Oh, damn.* He pulled me closer, nearly on top of his lap, and ravaged my mouth. It wasn't just his lips or his tongue, or even the way he took control. It was his hands, the brush of his fingers over my collarbone. It was the press of his hard body against mine. It was his low groan. *Shit*, it was just him. He'd cast a spell on me, made me want to be his for the night. Or for all the nights. Just one taste, and I wanted it all. His touch, his kiss, his dick. Everything.

All too soon, though, he pulled away and placed another searing kiss to my forehead. "*That* was PDA." The low rasp of his voice made me dizzy with need. He picked up the menu and muttered something about chocolate brandy mousse.

While he talked about drinks and dessert, I thought about his mouth. That kiss. And the fact that I'd let him do it, that I wanted him to do it again, that I'd whimpered when he'd pulled back, like a fucking baby. It would be futile to argue with him or even try to pretend it didn't happen.

"Indeed," I admitted finally. "That was definitely PDA." And *damn him*…I liked it. "I want the crème brûlée."

Chapter Eight

THE TRUTH

Preston

My thumb hovered over the SEND button. I'd drafted the email to Parker Wells Jr. a few days ago, requesting a meeting to discuss what I'd learned. After several edits, I still wasn't ready to send. The uncertainty kept me from opening the door to the possibility that Parker Wells Sr. was my biological father.

The DNA test was the easy part—only two possible outcomes. Yes, he was my father. Or no, my mother was just a liar. If he wasn't, my life would go back to normal. But if he was… *What effect will a bombshell like this have on my life?* No matter what people said, the truth didn't always set someone free. Sometimes the truth was just another form of prison, another life sentence of pain and misery.

"What are you doing here?"

Closing my email app, I set my phone down and looked at my mother. When I'd arrived early this morning, intent on hashing this out, she'd been asleep. Surprisingly, the house was clean. There was no evidence of hard partying, no empty liquor bottles. It reminded me of the times she'd come home from rehab with a "new lease on life," determined to get back on track. Those good times had never lasted, but they were some of my favorite memories of her.

"You're not hungover," I said. "You haven't been drinking."

"No, I haven't," she admitted, flinging her legs off the side of the bed and lighting up a cigarette. "I'm taking a break."

I lifted a brow. "Forever?"

She rolled her eyes at me. "Nunya."

Mom had tried to convince me I should be grateful that I had the *fun* mother. She often said that other kids had strict parents, mothers who monitored their every move and fathers who'd beat them. She'd even encouraged me to call her by her first name because she wanted to be my friend. Then, she'd get angry when I insisted on calling her Ma. I wanted someone to care about my homework and my grades. I wanted a mother who'd go to parent-teacher conferences—sober—and sports tournaments. I needed someone who concerned herself with *my* wellbeing, my failures, my successes. I just needed her to be my mother.

I stood and paced the floor slowly. The faint creek of the wood beneath my feet was the only sound as I pondered my approach. I felt her eyes on me, watching me. Waiting. Finally, I turned to her. "You said something to me the last time I was here."

She met my gaze unflinchingly. "I told you your father wasn't your father."

I studied her face, the hard line of her mouth and her

frosty glare. Times like this, I wondered if she'd ever loved me, because she damn sure didn't act like she even liked me. "Is it true? Was Hayes my father?"

"Did he raise you?" she asked.

"That's not what I asked you."

"Did he take you to baseball practice, teach you how to ride a bike?"

I clenched my teeth, massaging the back of my neck. She ticked off more activities—the time Hayes took me to the zoo, and when he'd chaperoned my one and only cub scout camp. The more she talked, the angrier I got. "Enough," I snapped.

Mom took a puff of her cigarette and blew the smoke out slowly. "It doesn't matter who your father is. Hayes was the man who was there for you."

"Right. He showed up every other weekend," I muttered dryly, "and sometimes at Christmas or Father's Day—when you would let him." I didn't want to get into how she'd micromanaged my relationship with him from the moment they'd separated. To steer this conversation back to the matter at hand, I asked, "Who is my father? Just answer the damn question."

"Your father is who I say your father is."

"Is Parker Wells Sr. my father?"

Mom's eyes widened. "What did you say?"

"You heard me. Parker Wells Sr. Is he my father?"

My mother stood, hastily pacing back and forth, muttering something incoherent under her breath. "Who told you that?"

"Is it true?"

She grabbed her robe off a chair and pulled it on. "I'm not talking about this." She tied the silk fabric at her waist and stomped toward the closet.

I followed her, stood near her but not too close. I needed to keep my distance. "Tell me."

"It doesn't matter." Dropping to her knees, she opened her trunk and tossed pieces of clothes behind her. She was looking for her stash. *Interesting.* The mere mention of the man had made her run for the liquor.

"Ma?" I touched her shoulder.

She jerked away from me. "Stop. Just…no." She pulled out a full bottle of Tito's, opened the top, and took a big gulp.

I dropped my head. In the back of my mind, I knew it was true. From the moment she'd told me, I'd felt it. And my mother's reaction had confirmed it. Even if she didn't know for sure, *she* thought Mr. Wells was my father.

She shuffled toward the recliner in the corner of the room and plopped down on it. Then, she took another sip from the bottle. "This conversation is over." She held up the bottle. "See what you made me do?"

"Don't put that on me. You could've just as easily drank a bottle of water."

She leaned her head against the cushion and stared out the window. "News flash. Parker is dead, anyway, so it really doesn't matter."

"You would've never even told me there was a possibility I had a different father."

"I told you what you needed to know." She shrugged. "That's all."

"You've manipulated me my entire life." And I'd let her, even after I was old enough to know better.

The late-night calls begging for money, the guilt trips for not being there when she needed me, and the emotional distance she'd insisted on keeping between us had done irreparable damage through the years. I didn't have to spend hundreds of dollars on therapy to know that being Kenya Hayes' son had somehow tarnished my life. The notion that I could have a healthy, committed romantic relationship had died a long time ago. Any hope for a semblance of normalcy seemed like a far-off dream, not even possible in light of my past. I'd spent so much of my time building walls to protect myself from more pain, more anguish, that I didn't even know if I *could* fall in love.

She snorted. "Please, you put me through some shit too. Always getting in trouble, going to court."

I would be the first to admit I wasn't perfect. Never pretended to be anything but me. I had to fight to keep from getting my ass kicked in the streets. I had to beat the shit out of many of her boyfriends just to get them off her. And I wasn't proud of it, but I had to steal to eat some days. Yes, I had an anger problem, but I fully believed that stemmed from the things I'd had to see, the things I'd had to do to protect her and to stay alive.

"I wonder why," I said, sarcasm dripping from my words. "It's not like I had a good example. Instead of acting like my mother, you alternated between treating me like your nuisance or your man."

Her expression hardened. "I took care of your little ass." She stood and stalked toward me. "I gave up my life for you."

I let out a humorless chuckle. "You never let me forget it, either. You never passed up a chance to tell me how great your life was before you got pregnant with me. And when exactly did you take care of me? Between stints in rehab and abusive boyfriends?"

The sting of her palm against my cheek startled me. I took a reflexive step back, but she slapped me again. And again. While she hit me, the liquor in her bottle splashed in my face, on my clothes. I tried to snatch the vodka from her, but her grip was tight.

When I finally wrestled it from her grasp, I held it up. "And this? This is more important to you than I ever was." I tossed it behind her. The glass crashed to the floor, shattering on the hard wood.

"Get out." She swung at me again, but I easily dodged the contact. "This is my house," she sneered. "And I don't want you here."

My throat went dry as anger pulsed through me. And since I'd never raise my hand to her or any other woman, I pounded my fist into the wall. The hole I'd left there would be a reminder of what she'd done and why this was the last time she'd ever be able to get under my skin. Straightening my shoulders, I glared at her. "Actually, this is *my* house. I'm the one who pays the bills here. I'm the one who takes care of you." I wiped my face with the back of my hand and stared down at my wet palm. "But you're right, it's time I get the fuck out of here."

She squeezed her eyes shut. Reaching for me, she took a step forward. "Preston."

I backed away and lifted my hand up. "Don't touch me. I love you. But I..." I let out a shaky breath. "I can't do this anymore."

"Do what? I'm trying to get better. It's not my fault. You just piss me off."

I raised a brow. "Piss you off? Wow."

"You're always judging me, making me feel like I'm nothing."

"You make yourself feel like nothing. Ma...*Kenya*, you need help."

She winced as if I'd smacked her. "Preston...babe? You can't do this. You have to understand—I'm not myself."

"You're definitely yourself." I pulled out my wallet and handed her two hundred dollars. "For groceries. I noticed you didn't have anything in the refrigerator." I walked out of her bedroom.

"Preston!" she shouted, following me, grabbing my arms to keep me there. I kept going, all the way to the front door. "Please." I paused, my hand on the doorknob. "I'm sorry." She was crying now, but I didn't turn to look at her. Because I knew what would come next. The begging, the promises to stay sober. "Forgive me."

It felt like my heart had cracked open. The pain was so consuming, I couldn't catch my breath. For once, though, I was going to put myself first, even if I had to walk away from my own mother. Lowering my head, I sucked in a deep breath and left.

Dallas

"WHO IS the hottie in the picture? #SendMeOneOfThem #Dayum" *Scroll.*

"Yasmin needs to whoop that ass for effing wit' her man. Kimball + Yasmin FOREVA!" *Scroll.*

"Sources say Kimball is divorcing Yasmin? Does she have something to do with that?" *Scroll.*

"That Bitch! She's a homewrecker!" *Report.*

"Who cares! This isn't news." *Like.*

"Kimball Payne is a punk with his little whining ass self. Maybe he should try scoring a touchdown. Dallas is better off without him. Go girl." *Love.*

"She's beautiful. I'm down for a threesome." *Block.*

Annoyed, I closed my Facebook and opened Twitter. I probably shouldn't have been checking social media right now—or ever again. I should've been working or drinking. Anything other than reading the comments about me and Kimball, me and my homewrecker status, me and mystery guy, me and anything that didn't matter.

After a quick scroll down my timeline, I blocked several people and posted a GIF of a woman looking bored, along with the caption #unbothered. The good news was I wasn't trending anymore. The bad news was I had a ton of mentions because one of the paparazzi had managed to snap a pic of Preston and I leaving Real Seafood Company after our dessert. Fortunately, it was an innocent photo, but it still made the rounds.

The interest in my love life was astounding. I wasn't a celebrity. I hadn't published any viral articles like Blake. I wasn't a celebrity chef like Duke. I didn't traipse all over the world giving seminars to couples and parents. And I definitely hadn't introduced a line of sex toys. I was just me, plain old Dallas. I loved my under-the-radar life, which was why I'd been very careful about who I associated myself with. I'd only dated two professional athletes in my life, and one of them was Kimball. The other was... I was just ready to get back to normal.

My phone buzzed, alerting me to a new message—from Kimball.

Dumb Ass: *Hey beautiful.*

More proof that he was a dingaling. No originality, no sense. I almost didn't respond. It wouldn't be the first time I'd ignored his ass. He'd been texting me nonstop for the past few days, right around the time those pics of me with Preston hit the web. I had time today, though. My response was brief: *Fuck you, Muthafucka.*

I set my phone down on the table, but picked it up again when my watch beeped. Smiling, I accepted the video chat request. Burrowing into the sofa, I grinned. "When are you coming to save me, Skye?"

"Girl, delete that damn tweet. The last thing you need is more mentions." Skye Palmer-Starks owned Skye Light PR. She was one of the best in the business, but more importantly, she was one of the best people I knew.

Although we weren't related by blood, she was family. The enduring relationship we had with the Starks had sustained us through good and bad times. Jax Starks and his wife, Ana, were the official godparents for all eight of us. Uncle Jax and my father had grown up together and remained closer than brothers. Together with the Starkses and Reids, we'd gone on vacations, celebrated milestones, mourned losses, and had even lived in the same Brentwood, Los Angeles neighborhood for a time. We'd spent more time with them than we had with our actual relatives. Our lives were so intertwined that I'd had many of my firsts with them—from my first kiss to my first drink.

"Did you delete it yet?" she asked.

"No."

"Do it now. I guarantee you someone got a screenshot, but at least it'll be gone."

I reopened the app and deleted the tweet. "Done."

"Good." Skye was walking briskly through what appeared to be an airport.

I tucked my feet under my butt and sipped my glass of wine. "Where are you going?"

"Cali," she answered.

"So why are you FaceTiming me, then? You could've just sent a text."

"I wanted you to see my face when I told you to take that shit down." The noise that I'd heard faded away. "Okay, I'm in the Sky Club." She let out a deep breath. "I needed Garrett here to carry my bags." Skye had recently gotten engaged to Garrett Steele. They both worked to mitigate scandals for their wealthy clients, but he was a crisis management attorney. "Anyway, what's going on with you? Duke told me to call you. He said you fucked up."

I laughed. "Tell my brother to mind his."

"He's just worried about you," Skye said.

I nibbled on my thumbnail. "Are you?"

She rolled her eyes. "Nah, girl. You got this. I noticed you cozied up to some mystery man." She waggled her eyebrows. "Who is he?"

"That's Preston."

Frowning, she asked, "Who the hell is that?"

"Cooper's friend. My friend. I don't know." I cracked up. "He's somebody."

She lifted a questioning brow. "Somebody you like?"

I didn't even bother answering that question because it was irrelevant. "Did Duke tell you I'm thinking of running for office?"

"He did," she replied. "He also told me something about a law organization?"

"Right. My mentor approached me about taking a leadership role in the org. They would then put their resources behind me for an eventual campaign."

"That's amazing, Dallas."

"Thanks. After that Kimball debacle, though, there was some concern that I wasn't the right pick. Preston agreed to help me out, attending events and such."

"Great. So, he's your good publicity. I like that. And since you didn't answer my question earlier, I'm going to assume you like *him*."

"It's just business. A favor."

Skye smirked. "Not sure I believe that, but okay."

"Why don't you believe me?"

"Because I know you. And I know that look on you."

I swallowed. "It's not that."

"Whatever you say, sis. I told Duke you didn't need me, though. You're already doing what I was going to suggest. A public relationship with someone *not* Kimball Payne will work. Just no dramatic breakups. Adults can and do end relationships all the time without fanfare."

"I know. It won't be like that."

"Although, I would've suggested doing this with someone else."

"I didn't want to do it at all," I told her. "But then someone snapped a picture of us in front of my house, and the rumor mill went crazy."

"What was he doing at your house? Before you say it was innocent, don't try it."

I shot her a mock glare. "I can't stand you, heffa."

She laughed. "You love me."

"You're lucky I do, because I would've cussed your ass out."

"So…?"

"He's cool." I shrugged. "We're sorta friends."

"You had sex with him, didn't you?"

I gaped. "No. I mean…not recently."

"I knew it!" She did a fist pump. "I'm so damn good. I figure shit out. Does Duke know?"

I thought about the immediate aftermath of my bathroom tryst with Preston, and how Duke had correctly surmised that I'd been fucking. "What do you think?"

Skye giggled. "Yeah, that's Duke. Always knowing shit."

"And never afraid to let you know that he knows," I added.

"That part," she chirped.

"Anyway, it hasn't happened since then, and it's not going to happen."

"Okay."

"I hate when you say that."

The corner of her mouth curved up. "Hey, I'm just sayin'. But you know…it's always better to be honest with yourself at least."

"Girl, I'm—" A knock at the door interrupted my thought. Frowning, I stood. "Hang on."

"It's okay. I have to board in a few minutes. I'll keep an eye on things, and I'll be in touch if I need to."

"Thanks, Skye." I ended the call and walked to the door. *Speaking of my fake boyfriend…* I smoothed my hand over my clothes and checked out my reflection in a small mirror by the door. It was no use. My hair was a mess and my clothes were hanging off. Basically, I looked like warmed-over shit. But I opened the door anyway and forced a bright smile. "Preston, hey. I thought we weren't meeting up until later." The fundraiser I'd agreed to attend wouldn't start until seven.

Preston didn't meet my gaze. "Hey."

The first thing I noticed was the angry bruise on his jaw. Frowning, I pulled him into the house. "Are you okay?" He didn't answer me right away and he still hadn't made eye contact. "Preston. What happened?"

When he finally glanced at me, I gasped. My hand flew to my chest because… *Oh my God.* He was crying.

Chapter Nine

HALFCRAZY

Dallas

I'd mastered the art of the silent treatment right around the age of nine. I remember it like it was yesterday—what I had on, where I was. Duke had told Jonathan Matthews that I had the cooties. And I'd crushed on Jon so hard, it felt like my world was ending. To make matters worse, Jon spread the rumor in school. Embarrassed was an understatement. I was humiliated.

I didn't speak to Duke for seven days. By the time that week was over, Duke was begging me to talk to him, and Jonathan was pleading with me to forgive him. While I'd eventually relented and let my brother back into my good graces, I never talked to Jon again. Not years later when he gave me a bouquet of pink carnations during the eighth-grade formal. Not even when he took out an "I apologize" ad in the high school yearbook.

Yet, as good as I was with giving the silent treatment, I

hated when someone gave it to me. *Hate it.* For instance, it'd been half an hour since Preston had shown up at my door and he'd said no more than three words. *No* and *Thank you.*

"Are you hungry?" I asked after another long moment of silence.

He shook his head.

"Okay," I murmured.

Thinking back, it occurred to me that Preston had been dealing with something for quite some time. My mind floated to the bar, the sad look in his eyes, his untouched shot of liquor. He hadn't talked about it then either, but I'd hoped he would. And now…I could see he wasn't in a good place. I could feel his anguish, his despair. The tears I'd seen in his eyes earlier were still there. I wanted to fix it.

"My mother is a drunk," he whispered.

My eyes flashed to him. Good thing I hadn't gone with my first mind and offered him a shot, but…*what do I say to that?*

His brows drew together, and a lone tear streaked down his face. "She's an addict who made my life a living hell." He glanced up at the ceiling. "I always tried to be there for her, to love her. I gave up pieces of myself to support her." Preston squeezed his eyes shut and more tears spilled on his cheeks. "Only for her to choose her vice, her liquor, over me time and again."

Oh shit, I'm crying too. I dashed a tear away.

His eyes bore into me, and I was struck by the intensity of his stare and the despair in his watery gaze. "I don't even remember her before she turned into what she is now." He stood and paced the floor like a caged animal. "I mean, I have *some* good memories, but they're wrapped in bad ones, because Sober Mom was never around long. And I'd have to pick up the pieces."

I peered up at him. "I'm sorry."

"What are you sorry for?"

I stood. "That you're hurting. I hate to see you like this." I inched closer and grabbed his hand. "I know I can't fix your mother, but I can be here to listen."

He rested his forehead on mine. Unsure what to do, I brushed the tears from his face, wrapped my arms around his waist, and hugged him. And he let me. We stayed like that for a moment.

When he pulled back, he offered me a small smile. "About tonight…"

I placed my finger over his lips. "Tonight is for you. The fundraisers and the galas can wait for another day."

He swallowed visibly, nodding. "Thanks."

Hours later, we were seated outside on my deck, drinking a glass of Merlot. Over the course of the day, he hadn't said much. I'd ordered pizza, which we ate while streaming the latest Marvel movie.

Watching the brilliant sunset against the beautiful Michigan sky was one of my favorite things to do. I loved the outdoors, the breeze against my skin, the sound of the wind rustling the trees, and even the rain. I felt most at peace when I was gardening or running through my favorite park.

"What is it like to have parents who were there for you, who accept you, who love you unconditionally?" he asked.

I tore my gaze from the evening sky and turned to him. I sensed he'd been struggling with what to talk about, and I was glad he'd said anything other than *Thanos was a punk* or *I'll take a slice of the bacon pizza.* "It's my greatest blessing," I answered. "I wouldn't be me without their influence and their love."

He stared at a point behind me. "I know this sounds crazy, but I used to wish my mom would go away. I thought if she left, I could go live with my aunt full-time—or my dad."

"Is that the aunt you were having brunch with?"

"Yeah. Aunt Dot."

"Where *was* your father?"

He let out a humorless chuckle. "Dead. Both of them."

Confused, I frowned. "Wait…"

"A couple of weeks ago, my mother told me the man I'd called Dad was not really my father."

Wow, that's fucked up. "Oh."

"Go ahead and say it," he commanded softly.

"Say what?"

"The first thing that came to mind when I told you that. That's fucked up?"

I blinked. It was uncanny how well he knew me but didn't really *know* me. I scratched the back of my neck. "Yeah, it is."

"She said it after I poured out one of her bottles of liquor."

"Is that why you were at the bar that day?"

He nodded. "Exactly."

"And why you didn't take your shot?" It made perfect sense to me that Preston had never finished his drink that night.

"I don't want to be like her," he admitted, "using liquor to numb my pain."

While my parents weren't big drinkers, their families were. Family reunions would often devolve into a fist fight or an argument because someone drank too much. It was one of the reasons we didn't spend time with our extended family. "I don't know your mother, but from the little bit you've shared, I don't think you're anything like her."

"You don't know that. Today, I went there to talk. But things went left. I got so angry. When she started hitting me, I couldn't control my rage. I punched a hole in the wall."

It was the first time he'd mentioned how he'd gotten the bruise on his jaw. "You didn't hit *her*. Show yourself some grace. You've been dealt a blow, Preston. Your world has been turned upside down. It's okay to *not* be okay."

He set his glass down on the ground. "I'm not."

"I get it. Can I ask you a question?"

"Go ahead."

"Did your mother tell you who your real father is?"

His eyes closed and he let out a slow breath. "No, but my aunt told me who it could be. And when I confronted my mother about it today, that's when things took a turn."

"You mentioned that both of your fathers are dead. So, the man who could be your father died too?"

"A few years ago. Apparently, he was a monster. A criminal, an adulterer, a liar..." His jaw tightened. "What does that make me?"

"It makes you Preston Hayes Jr. I know I said I wouldn't be who I was without my parents, but *you're* who you are *in spite of* your parents. What they've done or didn't do doesn't define you."

He stared at me. "You have that much faith in me?"

"Not really," I joked. "Just kidding."

"His name was Parker Wells Sr."

I frowned. "What?"

"Do you know him?"

"I know his kids."

He sat up. "Really? How do you know them?"

I explained the connection. Blake's good friend, Ryleigh, had married Martin Sullivan, who owned a business with Carter Marshall, who was married to Brooklyn Wells. I'd actually hung out with them a couple of times and had even visited Wellspring. "It's a small world."

"It is. Will you do me a favor?" Preston asked if I could contact Brooklyn. He wanted to meet with her and her brothers.

I agreed to call her first thing in the morning. "I'll let you know when I hear back from her."

He relaxed against the chaise again. "Thanks for this," he murmured.

I looked over at him and smiled. "No need to thank me."

"No, really. You didn't have to open your home to me, let me cry on your shoulder, or agree to help me."

"Why wouldn't I? I might be unengaged sometimes, but I'm not rude."

He laughed. "I guess not."

"Don't get too comfortable, though, because I might not like you next week."

Preston snickered. "I guess I should be grateful, huh? Does this mean we're friends now?"

"I…" My mouth fell open. "What? Why would you say that?"

He eyed me skeptically. "Don't think I don't know you like to call me your sorta friend."

Shit. I feigned innocence, placing a hand to my chest. "Me? Who told you that?"

"No comment."

I made a mental note to kick Coop the next time I saw him. "Okay, you got me. I don't make friends easily," I confessed.

"No, really?" The sexy smirk on his lips let me know he was being sarcastic.

I tossed a throw pillow at him. "Seriously. It's no small feat that I let you in."

"Your house?" he asked.

I felt a blush work its way up my neck. I'd let him into

my body too. But I wasn't about to open that door again. "Of course."

"You still didn't have to help me."

"I did. Besides, you're my fake boyfriend." The word *fake* left a bad taste in my mouth. This thing between us felt too big for fake, but there wasn't another category for it.

"Is that what I am?"

I lifted a brow. "Is this a trick question?"

He smiled then. A real, full smile. And my stomach flipped. "No."

Finishing the rest of my wine, I stood. "I should probably clean up."

He followed me inside. "Heaven forbid you don't throw out the two paper plates from dinner."

"Oh! You got jokes. Does this mean I can stop being nice to you?"

Preston broke down the empty pizza boxes while I wiped the table down. "Now that you mention it, I actually prefer you to be nice-nasty."

I cracked up. "Nice *and* nasty?"

His smile faded and his gaze fell to my lips. "Or nice and naughty."

No matter what, do not kiss him.

Preston inched closer. The air around us changed, and my lighthearted mood faded to horny as hell under his hooded stare. "Dallas," he whispered. "I don't think you realize what tonight meant to me."

One night. One fuck. And I'd already had that, so this should be a non-issue. But *damn*, he smelled so good. The heat from his body made me want to lean into him, to wrap my arms—and my legs—around him.

"I know the fundraiser was important to you," he continued, "and I appreciate that you didn't hesitate to skip the event for me."

How about two nights, two fucks? I blew out a shaky breath. "I told you to stop thanking me. It's not necessary."

He brushed his hands up my arms, over my shoulders and neck, to my face. Every touch of his fingers ignited something inside me. I was helpless, lost in my desire for him. "You're so beautiful." He circled my nose with his. "So damn sexy."

I shuddered as his words washed over me. The ability to reason with myself flew out the window. When he'd come to me, I'd wanted to ease his pain. Now I wanted something else. Him. Naked. Now. "Please," I gasped when he tugged me closer, and my body crashed against his.

"Please what?"

I stepped on the tips of my toes and kissed him. Because…I wanted his lips on mine. And his body. I broke the kiss, cupping his chin in my palm. "Take my clothes off," I breathed. "And yours too."

Before I could tell him where I wanted him to take me, he wrapped one strong arm around my waist and set me on the countertop. His lips were everywhere—on my mouth, on my cheeks, on my ears, on my neck—as he pulled my shirt up and off. My pants were next, then my panties.

He rubbed his nose over my ear, then whispered, "Be very sure, Dallas."

My heart pounded in my chest. The question wasn't hard to answer, but my reply would definitely change the dynamic at play. I could stop this, and maybe our tentative friendship would remain intact. Or I could keep going and have a delicious orgasm.

"Dallas?" His hand slipped between my legs and his fingers brushed my clit.

Damn. My body burned with need, screaming its answer loud and clear before I whispered, "I'm sure."

Preston tugged his shirt off and dropped his pants. Seconds later, he was inside me. We made slow love, different from the first time. It was torture, really. Because I knew it couldn't last. It was so easy to lose myself in him, in *us*. It felt like we were destined to do this, meant to spend more nights like this. I let out a hoarse cry when I came, gasping for breath as my orgasm pulsed through me. Preston followed me over, moaning my name.

A moment later, he bit down on my shoulder gently and stood. Immediately, I missed his warmth and wanted to pull him back. So I did. I grabbed his wrist and tugged him forward, wrapping my legs around him.

He placed a sweet kiss to my lips. "Ask me to stay?"

The doorbell went off, startling me. "Shit," I muttered, sliding off the counter. "Who the fuck is that?"

Preston pulled on his jeans while I rushed to the other side of the kitchen island to grab my clothes. I scrambled to get dressed and hurried to the door. I peered through the peephole and rested my forehead against the door. Glancing back at him, I gave him a once-over to make sure he was fully dressed. He was. Then, I opened the door.

Demi shouted, "I'm here!" before she hugged me. "Why are you sweating?" She surveyed me. "And why are your pants on backward?"

I looked down at my pants. "Um…"

She brushed past me. "I figured I'd surprise you, because you need my… Oh, damn." My best friend looked at me, then Preston. "I probably should've called first."

He greeted Demi and walked toward me. "I'd better go."

In the background, Demi pointed at Preston and

started twerking. I rolled my eyes at her and faced him. "Okay."

Leaning closer, he whispered, "Just so you know, we're not finished here."

I didn't comment on that. Instead, I patted his shoulder. "Drive safe."

He smirked. "Yeah, okay."

I watched him jog to his car. A moment later, I closed the door. *Three, two, one…*

"This is just business," Demi teased, mocking my stance from the beginning of this ruse.

I groaned. "Shut up." I stalked over to the kitchen and poured us both healthy glasses of wine. I handed her the glass. "I thought you weren't coming until tomorrow."

"I thought I'd come early to help my friend figure out her shit." Demi's eyes flickered with amusement as she sipped her Merlot. "But after what I just witnessed, I'm thinking you don't need me."

I padded over to the couch and plopped down. "We're not talking about this."

"Shiiiittt, we're definitely talking about this." She grabbed the bag of Chicago Mix popcorn on my counter and joined me on the sofa. "I need to know how you went from business to fucking." She froze. "I hope I'm not sitting in the wet spot."

I cracked up. "You're a damn fool."

She arched a brow. "Am I?"

I eyed her over the rim of my glass. "The wet spot is probably on the counter," I mumbled. *Note to self: Sanitize that countertop before bed.*

Demi stood up and did the running man. "Alright, nah. That's what I'm talking about." She fell back on the cushion. "Ooh." She blew out a breath. "That's not as easy as it once was."

"Girl, it was never easy."

She munched on the popcorn. "What *is* happening between you and Hottie Hayes?"

"Nothing. It was just a slip-up."

"Oh, so you just slipped on his dick?" She kicked off her shoes and tucked her feet under the blanket I kept on my sofa. "You're so full of shit."

"What? I had a lapse in judgment. I get one per year."

"Ah, so you're still full of shit." She took another sip. "It's okay, girlfriend. Good sex is always appropriate."

"I can't stand you."

"You love me."

Demi was right. I loved the hell out of her. We'd met during an Introduction to Fencing class right before my eleventh birthday and had bonded. While I'd enjoyed the sport, and had even competed, Demi had hated it. But we stayed friends, even after she'd quit and taken up swimming instead.

Earlier, I'd told Preston I didn't make friends easily. I meant that. When I met Demi, though, she'd offered me a level of acceptance that rivaled my own siblings. She understood me and had never tried to change me. I felt comfortable opening up to her, sharing things about myself that I couldn't tell anyone else. And vice versa. She was more than my friend. She was my sister, ranking right up there with Paityn, Blake, and Bliss.

We spent the next half an hour catching up from the last time we'd talked—which was earlier in the day. But it always seemed like so much life happened between our daily conversations.

"Okay, sis." Demi folded her arms. "You've managed to avoid this, but *dammit*, I want to know. It's not like you to backtrack, but you did with Preston. Does this mean you like him?"

"Today I did," I said matter-of-factly. "You've seen him. He's hot."

"Girl, yes he is." Demi reached over and gave me a high-five. "That ass."

"And those lips." Just thinking about his mouth made me want to kick Demi out and call him back over. "But he's just a friend."

"So, friends who fuck is a thing. We both have been there, done that. Yet, I'm sensing that isn't the case with him."

The fact that my best friend knew me so well was not shocking. *Annoying*, but not shocking. I wouldn't categorize what had happened between Preston and I as a simple friends-with-benefits arrangement. At the same time, I was hesitant to call it something more. "Well, it's not..." I let out a frustrated breath. "I don't actually know what it is. But it won't happen again."

"I don't doubt that you believe that. I'm just not sure *I* do."

I shrugged. "Well, watch me work. I know how to have sex and keep it moving."

"Not always," she countered.

I finished my glass of wine. "That isn't what this is."

"Isn't it?" She hugged her knees to her chest. "Babe, you know I think you're a rock star."

"But...?"

"I also think you're full of shit."

I gaped, hitting her with a pillow. "Will you stop staying that? I am not."

"Okay, maybe not full of shit. But you're definitely running."

"I told you, I'm not."

"Zeke died."

"Don't talk about him." I stood, marching back into

the kitchen and topping off my glass again. I gathered myself for a moment. The last thing I wanted to do was talk about Zeke. It had been five years since the accident that had claimed his life and I still felt the pain as if it were yesterday.

Demi walked over to me. "Fine, I won't say anything else—*after* I say this."

I met her gaze. "What?"

"You've been closing yourself off ever since he died. It's almost like you're punishing yourself for something you had no control over."

My vision blurred and my chest tightened. And my heart… The mere mention of his name always seemed to elicit this reaction, this searing ache in my chest, the overwhelming despair, and the crushing guilt. Ezekiel Reid. Our relationship had burned hot and heavy for years in secret, then had crashed and burned because I wasn't ready. I'd broken up with him the day he'd died in a car accident, and I'd regretted my actions every day since that fateful night. Because I *had* loved him, but I'd been too busy and too scared to do it publicly.

"I'm done with this conversation." I left her standing there and returned to my position on the sofa. "Enough about me, why are you staying so long?" She'd told me earlier she planned to stay in town for a couple of weeks.

Demi looked like she wanted to say more, but as always, she respected my wishes. "I'm actually thinking of moving back," she announced. A little over a year ago, Demi had made the decision to move her practice to the west coast. I always knew the decision was more about getting away from here than wanting to be in California. But I'd supported her anyway.

"Why?" I asked.

She picked at her fingernail. "It's hard, being away

from family." She scratched her temple. "From y'all, really."

Demi had grown up in the Metro Detroit suburb of Romulus, which was approximately twenty miles from Ann Arbor. Her parents had divorced when she was eight years old, after years of bitterness, abuse, and lies.

Her father was a partner at a top family law firm and had gained a reputation as the worst divorce attorney a woman could ever hire. Not that he'd take any woman's case, because Allan Strong only represented men. And he'd left a trail of destruction in his wake too. All because Demi's mother hadn't wanted him anymore. He was a bitter, angry man, who'd kept his only daughter from having a relationship with her mother. My friend had suffered for years until my mother had offered to take her in so she could attend Ann Arbor schools with us.

Under our roof, Demi had thrived and eventually decided to follow in her father's footsteps and become a divorce attorney. Only, she'd purposed to defend women against men like her father. Although she was in her early thirties, her skill in the courtroom had earned her a nickname—The Divorce Whisperer.

"Have you talked to Tyn about it?" I asked. Paityn and Demi lived close to each other and had often hooked up to hang out. "You do have *some* support there."

"And I'm grateful, but it's not the same." She put a handful of popcorn in her mouth. Once she swallowed, she said, "You can go ahead and tell me you told me so."

I pulled a throw over my legs. "I won't. I just think you should do what's best for you."

"I don't know why I thought leaving would help. It never does."

"True, but sometimes you have to leave so you can know that." The room descended into silence. "I do like

Preston," I confessed. "When I'm with him, I don't think of all the loss—or the guilt so much. I only think of him. And that scares me."

Demi squeezed my hand. "I get it, but you have to open yourself up sometime."

My friend had a point. Even still…I didn't know if I'd ever be able to fully open myself up again.

Chapter Ten

FEELS SO MUCH BETTER

Preston

Playing softball today. Veteran's Memorial Park.

I stared at the text, wondering whether I should consider this an invitation—or a test. Or both. It'd been seven days since Dallas had given me the best pussy I'd had in a long time. Probably ever, now that I thought of it. Of course, we'd seen each other—over FaceTime, at a luncheon, during a seminar, and at dinner. And nothing had really changed between us.

Once again, Dallas had reverted to her uninterested persona. The only difference was that she'd actively engaged me regarding my paternity situation and had stayed true to her word and reached out to Brooklyn Wells. But as far as the sex, not one word about it. In fact, she'd gone out of her way to put physical distance between us. Even at the events we'd attended, she'd kept our interactions very brief and mechanical. Which would've been fine had this happened a couple of months ago. This time, though, I didn't think I could pretend it'd never happened. I couldn't make myself forget how she'd taken care of me, how she'd listened. More importantly, there was no way to turn back the clock and take back everything I'd told her.

Opening myself up to her in the way I had was new for me. I'd never shared much about my mother or my childhood. Aunt Dot and Coop were the only people I'd confided in over the years. Aunt Dot because she was there, and Coop because he'd shown me I could trust him. And because I'd thought I was dying.

I could add Dallas to that short list now. Yet, I wasn't entirely sure she wanted to be part of the club. I glanced at the text message again. If I didn't reply, she wouldn't like it, because she *hated* being ignored. If I did reply…

A knock on the door pulled me from my thoughts. I'd driven to the Detroit office for an important meeting, and I needed to clear my mind from Dallas so I could focus on it. I locked my phone and answered the door.

The petite woman on the other side flashed a tentative smile. "Hi. Are you…?" She sucked in a deep breath and her shoulders dropped. "Shit, you are." She reached out and shook my hand. "I'm Brooklyn, and apparently you're my brother."

Frowning, I said, "Come in." Holding the door open, I waited until she entered my office. "Thanks for stopping by."

Brooklyn had reached out to me directly once she'd spoken with Dallas. Right away, she'd put my mind at ease with her sense of humor and her willingness to hear me out. The conversation had been brief, but she was friendly and not that surprised that I could be her brother. When she'd mentioned a two-hour layover in Detroit before her flight to L.A., she'd suggested we meet up.

"Can I get you anything?" I asked. "Water? Coffee?"

"No, thank you." She stared at me, grabbing the sides of her head. "I'm sorry, but…*damn*, you look like Senior." She blinked, her mouth falling open slightly. "I mean, you have his eyes, his nose. You even sound just like him. Well, except you seem nice."

Senior? "Is that what you called him?"

With her gaze still fixed on me, she nodded. "Yes," she murmured. "He insisted on it. You and Bryson…you look alike too."

I wanted to ask her more, quiz her on all the facts. I wanted to know about Bryson and Parker Wells Jr. I wanted to know *her*. My sister. *Potentially*. But we didn't have much time. "I hope this wasn't too much trouble, meeting me here."

She swallowed visibly. "No. I needed to see you for myself." Shrugging, she added, "I guess the paternity test is a formality at this point. If you're *not* my brother, I'd be shocked."

I agree. A couple of months ago, I was an only child, and now I had siblings. *Allegedly*. "I'd love to schedule a longer visit. I have several questions."

"The answers won't be nice. But if you're willing to listen, I don't mind sharing." She moved closer, searching my eyes. Her face softened. "I don't know what it's like to be you right now, but I do know how it feels to be disappointed, to be lied to. I can only hope things look up from here."

I cracked a small smile. "Thanks."

Brooklyn let out a deep sigh. "I didn't tell Parker, Ronnie, or Bryson that I was coming—or even that you'd contacted me. I thought it'd be best if I came first. Plus, Parker likes to control everything. Be warned."

Chuckling, I said, "Got it."

"I'll set up sibling testing. Maybe we can go to a nearby lab when I come back to Michigan? Once we know for sure, I'll tell them. It's better that way." She glanced at her watch. "Shit, I gotta go."

"Sounds good to me. Just let me know, and I'll make myself available."

Brooklyn held out her hand, yet let it fall to her side. She stepped forward, but retreated backward. She opened her arms, then hugged herself. "Ah, forget it." And she hugged me. "I'm a hugger," she whispered. "You'll get used to it."

I didn't know this woman, had never seen her before today, but my instincts told me she was sincere. Something told me that once Brooklyn made her mind up about anything, she was a force to be reckoned with. But I could also sense she'd be a great person to have in my corner.

When she pulled back, she shot me a soft smile. "I'm kind of bossy as well," she confessed. "You'll get used to that too."

I barked out a laugh. "As long as you get used to my quiet moods."

A corner of her mouth quirked up. "That won't last long. We're a pretty loud bunch." She walked to the door. "I'll be in touch."

"I look forward to it."

Turning back to me, she said, "Bye, Preston."

Just like that, she was gone, her face still registering the shock I felt. I worked for about an hour after Brooklyn left, but decided it was futile. I couldn't concentrate on anything other than the upcoming DNA test. So, I'd made the forty-five-minute drive to Ann Arbor.

At Veteran's Memorial Park, I located the baseball diamond where Dallas and her family played, and parked near it. As I approached the field, I immediately spotted

Blake on first base. On the pitcher mound, Dexter stood, eyes on the hitter. But…*where is she*? I peered into the dugout and noticed the rest of her clan. She wasn't there, though. I checked my phone to see if I'd missed a text or a call. Nothing.

Seconds later, Dexter tossed the pitch. The batter swung, connecting with the ball. On third base, Mr. Young shouted commands at Asa, who was at second base. The play was fast. Tristan picked up the ball and tossed it to Asa, who tossed it home. The catcher jumped up, caught the ball, and tagged the opposite team's runner.

"Out!" the umpire called, extending three fingers signaling it was the third out.

Blake did a fist pump and held her hands up to her face like a makeshift megaphone. "You'd better catch that ball, Sissy. Yes!"

My gaze traveled back to the catcher, just in time to see Dallas pull the helmet off and drop it. "I got you," she yelled back. "That's game."

While the teams greeted each other with handshakes, I made my way to the dugout, where they were celebrating their win. Dallas looked radiant, helmet hair and all. Her eyes were bright, her smile was genuine, and that body… still beautiful in her chest protector and leg guards.

"Hey, Preston!" Bliss waved at me.

Dallas whirled around and met my gaze. "Hey."

I gave Dex, then Tristan dap. Turning to her, I tipped my head. "What's up?"

She approached me. "I didn't think you were coming?"

Lifting a brow, I asked, "I didn't know I'd received an invitation."

I could've imagined it, but it looked like she smiled. "Touché." She sighed. "Walk with me?" I followed her to a grassy knoll on the opposite end of the diamond. Once we made it there, she sat on the ground. One of the things I loved about Dallas was she wasn't afraid to be outside, to get dirty. She enjoyed the outdoors as much as I did. "Join me?"

I sat next to her. "What's up, Dallas?"

"How did it go with Brooklyn today?"

For a second, I'd forgotten I'd mentioned I would be meeting Brooklyn today. It did something to me that she remembered and wanted to know how it had gone. I gave her a quick rundown of my introduction to my *maybe* sister. "She's going to schedule a DNA test when she gets back to town."

Dallas hugged her knees to her chest and picked at a piece of grass. "How do you feel about everything?"

I hunched a shoulder. "I don't know. Overwhelmed. Apprehensive. Excited." It hadn't occurred to me that it'd be a *good* thing my father was Parker Wells Sr. when I'd found out it was a possibility. After meeting Brooklyn, though, I realized it might not be so bad to have sisters and brothers. "It's a lot," I added. "Hard to say how I'll feel once it's confirmed—or not."

"Well, you have some time to adjust. I just want you to be okay." She rolled her eyes and shook her head. "That's all."

I smirked. "Was it really that bad to say that?"

Her surprised gaze met mine. "I really need to watch my reactions around you." She laughed. "I don't have this problem with many other people."

"Why is that?"

She frowned. "Why don't I have this problem?"

I shook my head. "Why *do* you have this problem with me?" I clarified.

Dallas averted her eyes. "Honestly, I have no idea."

I leaned over, bumping my shoulder against hers to get

her attention. When she looked at me, I said, "I think we should talk about it."

Her eyes widened for a second before she schooled her features. "About what?"

"About this?" I motioned between us. "And the reason why we've had sex two times and have yet to discuss it."

"Do we have to?" The tiny crease in her brow was too cute to ignore. I brushed my thumb over it, then trailed my forefinger down the bridge of her nose. "You're touching me again."

I barked out a laugh. "So?"

"Maybe we should establish ground rules."

"I think we've already fucked that up, right? Literally."

She smacked my arm. Giggling, she said, "That was so damn corny."

"By design." The awkward pause that followed my words pissed me off. "Let's not do this."

"Okay," she grumbled. "Damn. I'm not this weird normally."

"I know that, which is why I'm confused."

"Believe it or not, I've never been in this position before. Sex isn't usually this complicated."

"What's so complicated? You do it, then you're done."

She gaped. "You know it's not that simple."

I absolutely knew it wasn't simple, but it didn't have to be hard either. "Why? Look, I enjoy you. And I don't think we have to make this a huge deal. We're both capable of keeping boundaries. At the same time, we have to spend time together, so wouldn't it be best if we took advantage of that?"

"As in…?"

A smile tugged at my lips. "As in, let's not be awkward with it. As in…how about we not pretend we aren't attracted to each other? As in sometimes friends fuck."

"Who said you were my friend?" She grinned. "Just kidding. You're right." Dallas placed her hand on my knee. "Can I add an 'as in' to this thing?"

I raked my gaze over her face, lingering on her eyes, then the little dirt spot on her cheek. I brushed my finger over it, wiping it away. Her eyes fluttered closed. "Definitely," I murmured.

Dallas blew out a shaky breath. "As in let's not assume we'll actually have sex again?"

"Do you really think we won't?"

"Um…" She nibbled on her bottom lip. "That's not the point." She laughed. "I'm pretty sure it's a foregone conclusion, but I would like the record to show that we agreed to this."

"Fine," I said.

"Oh." She held up one finger. "Another one…as in still no public displays of affection."

My gaze dropped to her mouth. "Sure?"

She gripped my collar and pulled me closer, murmuring against my ear. "I'm sure."

I pulled back. "Oh, so you're just going to do me like that?"

"Yep." She stood up and brushed her pants off. "I have to go. Double header. Next game starts in a few minutes." She grinned. "Want to try on the spare uniform?"

I got up. "Nah, I'm good."

She walked toward her group. "I think you're scared." Turning to me, she grinned. "No, you're scurred." Then, she took off.

An hour later, I was lying flat on my back in the grass after a fly ball hit me in the head. Dallas stood over me, her hand covering her smile. "Don't say anything," I murmured.

"What?" She shrugged. "I thought you realized your job was to *catch* the ball, not block the ball with your head."

"The sun got in my eyes," I lied. "Blinding, really."

It was a wrap from the time I'd jogged out on the field until now. Softball had never been my game. But I wasn't about to admit that in front of her family. It had started well enough. I'd missed the first ball hit to me, but I'd recovered nicely, tossing the ball to Dallas, who was playing first base this game. She'd caught it easily and had tagged the runner out. But the next time, I'd thrown the ball to the wrong base, which had resulted in a score for the other team. And when I'd gone up to bat, I struck out.

Dallas' lips formed a dramatic sad face. "Aw, poor Lil' Tink Tink."

"Don't do me," I said.

She laughed. Again.

"Damn, Pres." Dex scratched his head. "I thought you were athletic."

Hell, I thought I was too. Until I realized softball wasn't as easy as I'd thought it would be. *Why did I let Mr. Young convince me to take his spot in center field?* "Man, shut the hell up. I didn't have the right shoes on." Or the right glove. Or the right skills.

"Son—" Mr. Young shook his head, "—that was pitiful."

Dex held out his hand. "Did you want me to help you up, or are you good?"

Dallas snorted. "It's okay to get help."

I swatted his hand away. "Move." I rolled over on my stomach and stood. Slowly.

"Are you okay?" she asked me. "Maybe you should go sit down."

I wrapped my arm around her and whispered against

her ear, "On second thought, I think I do need help. But only from you."

She beamed. "See? Was that so bad? It's always better to ask for assistance."

"Did you have to say that out loud?" I glanced over at Dex, who was pretending not to listen. Badly. "I have a rep to protect."

Dallas patted my stomach. "Sorry, Preston. It's too late for that rep." She laughed. "At least as far as softball goes." I squeezed her tightly, and she dissolved into more laughter. "Okay, okay. I'm done teasing." She brushed her thumb over my war wound. "And I got you. I'll let my family know I'm done and we can go."

Chapter Eleven

I WANT YOU AROUND

Dallas

The power of the human mind was really astounding. Words had power, yes. But thoughts could manifest weakness or greatness, happiness or sadness, sanity or insanity, revulsion or attraction. I'd experienced all of the above, often in the same day. But today? In a matter of hours, I'd run the gamut of those emotions as we'd golfed with Maya and her colleagues during their annual golf outing.

Due to our hectic work schedules, my four-day trip up north for the Young in Love retreat, and Preston's week-long business trip, I hadn't seen him in person since his unfortunate softball incident. Although we'd talked often, the physical distance had provided the perfect opportunity for me to reset, to recalibrate my expectations. Yet, when he'd arrived earlier, I'd been struck by two things—the way he looked in those navy golf pants and white polo, and the realization that I'd missed him. That awareness had set several things in motion—in my head, of course.

It all started when I nearly collapsed on the green after he'd given me a hug *and* a kiss in front of everyone. And I almost begged him to take me behind a tree—or something. I refrained from making a fool out of myself, but Preston was relentless. Being all sexy and shit, distracting me at every turn. Basically, he did everything we agreed he'd do in front of the ladies—acted like my doting lover. He carried my clubs, stood too close to me when he helped me from the golf cart, and offered me pointers on my game. Preston cheered me on when I made a good shot and encouraged me when I flubbed the ball. I found myself watching him, memorizing his movements, daydreaming about his mouth.

All morning, I warred with myself, ticking off the many *stupid* reasons I wanted to keep him at arm's length while simultaneously reasoning with myself about why it would be appropriate to have *three nights, three fucks*. Then, I teetered between irritation at him for making me like this and arousal because he was too damn close. I was getting on my own damn nerves.

Things had been going well for me with the org. Susan had invited me to her home for tea and conversation a couple of days ago. It definitely helped that the older women were taken with Preston. At this point, I was a shoo-in for membership. Which should've been cause for celebration, or at least a stiff drink. What was I doing instead? Glaring at Susan's daughter, Arlene, who'd shown up unannounced and had promptly homed in on *my* fake boyfriend.

Right now, all I wanted to do was push Arlene's lyin' ass in the pond. Not that I could talk, considering Preston wasn't really my man, but at least I didn't make a habit out of pretending. Arlene hadn't even bothered to hide her interest in Preston, so she'd *pretended* to be golf illiterate. Never mind she knew all the golf terms and had her own set of clubs. Never mind her mother had already bragged about Arlene's golf awards during our tea. Next, Arlene had *pretended* to sprain her ankle so Preston could help her to her golf cart. Then, her Treasure-troll-looking ass *pretended* to be interested in hiring him as a consultant for a construction project.

If Bliss were here, she'd be quick to point out my jealousy, but since she wasn't, I happily blamed my mood swings on Arlene. Because...*what the hell?* When did two fucks and a couple of conversations make me a jealous bitch?

"Are you okay, sweetie?" Maya whispered as we packed up our stuff.

"I'm fine," I grumbled.

Maya giggled. "You're definitely *not* fine."

I lifted my bag. "Actually, I am."

"Dallas." She hugged me, "It's okay to like him for real, ya know?"

"I don't," I said. "I mean, I do. We're friends."

"I got this." Preston took my bag from me and slung it over his shoulder.

Where the hell did he come from? I wondered if he'd heard me. I glanced at Maya, catching her knowing smile. "I'm fine," I repeated, stomping off.

When we returned to the clubhouse, the ladies suggested we have lunch.

"Aw, I wish I could," I said.

"Sounds good," Preston agreed.

Our simultaneous responses annoyed the hell out of me. I shot Preston a glare and mumbled, "But we have that thing."

Preston went along with me. "Right. That *thing*."

We exchanged small talk with the ladies while they waited for their table. Once they were ready to be seated, I hugged Maya and said my goodbyes to the other ladies. Well, everyone except for Arlene. I was too busy fighting not to kick her in the butt when she gave Preston a hug that lasted one second too long.

"Thanks for today," I mumbled when they disappeared into the building. Shame rolled through me like waves. I'd never come close to reacting that way about any man. Not even Zeke.

Preston smirked. "Are you good?"

"What do you think?" I snapped.

He glanced at his phone and his smile faded. "Can you give me a second?"

Now, I just felt like an asshole. "Sure. I hope everything is okay."

He excused himself and walked toward a bench on the other side of the walkway. I tried to eavesdrop on his conversation, but he was too far away for me to hear anything. So, I just stared at him. Preston was all hard lines and rippling muscles, haunted eyes and a genuine smile, quiet strength and dry humor. My brain screamed, *Girl, don't do it. Don't fall.* But my heart…that damn traitorous heffa. No matter how many times I told myself this wasn't an actual thing, my heart seemed to rebel against me.

The weird part was *he* hadn't changed. He'd been the same Preston I'd always known. Calm, steady, smart, thoughtful, fine. He was always a gentleman, shielding me from strangers and making sure I wasn't cold. Those things…one might think they were small in the grand scheme of life. Yet, somehow, the simple gestures, the fleeting moments of understanding between us, had become promises. The promise to protect me, to care for me, to listen to me. The more time I spent with him like this, the more I wanted to be near him. Which could become a problem when this charade was over.

"Dallas?"

The butterflies fluttering in my stomach a second ago were replaced with cold, hard dread at the sound of the male voice calling my name. Kimball. I sighed, then turned to face him. "What the hell do you want?"

Kimball glanced over my shoulder, presumably at Preston. "Who is that? The man you were with."

I scanned the area. The media attention had died down somewhat since the ruse had started, and I didn't need more fodder for the reporters to latch on to. "Does it matter?"

"I've seen you with him," he said. "The pictures. Who the fuck is that?"

"Shut the hell up," I hissed. "Take your ass somewhere else. It's your fault my name is being dragged for filth in these streets."

Kimball shifted from one foot to another. "I've been calling you."

"Right. I thought I made myself very clear in my last text. Just in case you need a reminder, here's one. Fuck you, muthafucka. Find your wife and leave me the hell alone."

"Everything okay over here, baby?" Preston's hand slid over my back. "Are you alright?"

The flutters were back stronger than ever. Just his touch, his scent… *Ooh wee.* I took a steadying breath and forced a smile. "I'm fine."

"Dallas, we need to talk," Kimball said, stepping toward me.

Preston stood between us. "Nah, that's not how this is going down. I believe she told you to leave her alone. You might want to do that, because I'd hate the media to get a clip of me beating the shit out of you at this country club."

Well, damn. Kick-ass Preston could get it. But the longer we stood here, the more likely we would be spotted. I squeezed his arm. "Can we go?" I whispered.

Nodding, Preston said, "Definitely."

"I meant what I said," I told Kimball. "We're done."

Kimball stalked off like a spoiled toddler, complete with a pout and folded arms.

Once he was out of sight, I sighed. "Thanks for the save." When Preston didn't respond, I turned to him to find him staring at the spot where Kimball had disappeared. "Preston? You okay?"

He squeezed his eyes shut and blew out a harsh breath. "I'm fine." His expression softened. "Are you?"

I slipped my hand in his and pulled him toward his truck. "Kimball's an asshole. That's it. But I'm not worried about him. My concern is you. What happened?"

He dropped his head. "Got the paternity test." I held my breath and waited for him to speak. Finally, he peered up at me. "Parker Wells Sr. is my father."

"Oh." I sighed heavily. I knew Preston and Brooklyn had agreed to do a DNA test, but I hadn't expected the results to come back so quickly. "That was Brooklyn?"

"Yeah," he replied. "She received the results and called me right away."

"When did you take the test?"

"A couple of days ago when I got back from South Carolina. We went to a local lab when she returned to Michigan."

"That worked out." I searched his eyes, noted the sadness within them. "How are you feeling about it?"

"I don't really know how to feel," he admitted.

I held out my hand. "Understandable. So how about

you don't think about it tonight?"

He narrowed his eyes on me. "Not sure that's possible."

"Maybe not, but we can try." I held out my hand. "Come with me?"

Without hesitation, he slipped his hand into mine and smiled. "Lead the way."

PRESTON LEANED OVER AND MURMURED, "Do they always do this?"

I glanced at Tristan and Duke, who were engaged in a full-blown argument about the rules of the game, Taboo—which we'd been trying to play for the past half hour. I shrugged. "Pretty much."

Duke shoved Tristan. "Back up, man. Take your fun-killin' ass somewhere else."

Tristan bopped Duke in the head. Then, they were fighting.

Preston stood, but my hand on his wrist pulled his attention back to me.

"They're fine," I said. "Don't get in the middle." He looked at me, a question in his eyes. I waved a dismissive hand toward my brothers. "Seriously. Just let them go at it."

After we'd left the golf course, Preston had followed me to my house so I could change. Then, we'd headed to my parents' house for Tristan's birthday dinner. Duke had flown in for the occasion and treated us to a smorgasbord of dishes that included perfectly grilled steak and salmon, pulled pork with his special barbecue sauce, coleslaw, seafood pasta salad, corn on the cob, strawberry shortcake, and other treats.

Now that all of my siblings were adults with our own

careers and relationships, spending time together had become extremely important. We wanted to maintain a closeness despite what was going on in our lives. For a while, Tristan had been absent on purpose, often choosing to forego family events even if he was available. My big brother's unwillingness to be involved in certain celebrations and his ability to make everything serious had always rubbed Duke the wrong way. So there'd been a constant battle between the two of them for years. It wasn't uncommon for them to fight—with their words or with their fists.

Preston stared at my brothers, who were now rolling around on the grass. "Okay."

I smirked at my fake boyfriend. Preston was a protector, the calm person in the room, and I knew it must've been hard for him to deal with the fight. The fact that he'd been ready to break it up made my heart swell in appreciation for the man he was. Not many would be willing to jump into a family disagreement.

My mother stepped onto the deck with chips and homemade guacamole. She shook her head. "Not again." She looked at Dex. "Get them."

"Alright now, that's enough." My father's soft voice sounded like a boom in the backyard. Tristan and Duke immediately froze, fists in the air. All conversation ceased. We called it the Dad Effect. No matter what we were doing, when he spoke, we listened. He never had to yell, because his simple presence packed a punch.

Tristan stood. "Sorry, Pop." He held out his hand and pulled Duke to his feet. "You know how it is."

My dad set a tray of veggies and dip on the table. "Actually, I think it's time for you two to do a deeper dive into what's fueling this animosity."

Duke shrugged. "I don't need to think about it. I

already know. Tristan's full of shit."

My mom held out her hand, and Duke smacked a twenty-dollar bill into her palm. My mother had made quite a bit of money on our propensity for well-placed curse words. Even though none of us lived with them anymore, the Cussing Jar was still active. "Thank you," she chirped. "I'll be able to pay for my spa date after tonight."

"You should be able to pay for a vacation to Jamaica," Blake grumbled.

"I'm just sayin'," Duke said. "We all know it. Right, Demi?"

I glanced at my best friend, who'd averted her gaze from the melee.

She met Tristan's gaze but didn't say anything. "Don't bring me into this," she warned.

"Duke, sit your ass down," I ordered, pulling out a bill and handing it to my waiting mother. "This is neither the time nor the place for this. We have company." The past between Demi and Tristan often made family gatherings uncomfortable for them. I didn't want it to ruin the rest of the night.

Duke snorted. "I don't see any company. Lennox is family, and Preston isn't new to us either. But since we're talking about deeper dives, don't you all think it's time for Tristan to deal with his shit? It's about—"

Dad shot Duke the look, and my brother shut the hell up, excusing himself and walking inside the house.

Tristan stalked off toward the private lake and, surprisingly, Demi followed him.

Dex sighed. "Shit," he grumbled, setting his beer on the table. A moment later, he headed into the house.

Sighing, I turned to Preston. "Sorry. My family is…"

"Yours. And here." He placed his hand on my knee. "Do you want to go in after him?"

I glanced at the door, then back at Preston. Nodding, I went into the house. Blake was right behind me.

My parents' house sat on five acres of land and was located on the north side of Ann Arbor. They'd spared no expense to make it a place we could all come back to. Even though we lived separate lives, this house was always home. We found Duke in the basement, at the bar.

"Hey." I slid onto a bar stool next to Dex. "I hate that you two can't talk about this."

Blake leaned against the counter. "It's really tired, Duke."

Duke frowned. "Man, I'm sick of this shit. He comes into town and acts like he doesn't have to address anything. Mom and Dad go all out when he gets here, then he leaves without a word."

"Okay, but what does that have to do with you?" I asked. "He's not hurting you. Just let Tristan do him. And you continue to do you."

"You know better," Blake added. "So do better."

Dex drummed his fingers on the bar top. "Bottom line, Tristan has to work through his shit. We know that. But you don't have to make it your problem."

"Exactly," I agreed. "Just love him and be there for him when he finally needs us."

Duke dropped his head. "You're right. I'm just trippin'. I'll shut my ass up."

"Good." Blake looked at me. "So, Dallas…you and Preston hanging out when there's no Color of Law event?"

I shot her a sidelong glance. "It's complicated," I said with a shrug. "But, yes. We're friends."

"Not *sorta* friends?" Duke asked.

Preston and I had surpassed that sometime between the hot counter sex and that softball game. "No, we're friends."

Dex smirked. "That it?"

At this point, I was unwilling to admit anything more —to them or myself. "That's it," I repeated. "He's going through something, and I wanted to be there for him."

Blake sipped on the glass of cognac Duke had just poured her. "Is he okay?"

I didn't particularly want to discuss Preston's issues with my siblings, but I knew they'd keep my confidence, so I told some of what I knew about the paternity issue. "Brooklyn called him today with the results."

Blake's mouth hung open. "Whoa! That's a lot." Her brows furrowed. "But it makes sense. I knew he was too fine to be true. Those Wells brothers... Just hot for no good reason. Preston fits in perfectly."

I cracked up. "You're a nut."

"Seriously, though, they'll welcome him in."

I hoped she was right. It was totally different to meet a friend of a friend than meeting a long-lost sibling. The Wells family had already been there, done that when they'd discovered Veronica was their sister from another of their father's affairs. "Let's hope for the best." I stood. "I'd better get out there before Mom and Dad ask him too many questions."

I left my siblings in the basement and made my way back outside. When I stepped onto the deck, Preston was playing chess with my father. I leaned against the door and watched him. He was comfortable, engaged. And I was...*smitten*?

I inched toward them, placing my hand on Preston's shoulder. "All good out here?" I asked.

Preston peered up at me and nodded, before turning his attention back to the board.

Dad grinned. "I think Preston is miles better at this game than his softball game."

Laughing, I said, "That's a good thing, right?"

"I can see I'll never live this down," Preston said. "I might need to practice so I can redeem myself."

My father shook his head. "Son, sometimes it's better to let it go."

LATER, Preston walked me to my door. "Thanks for coming over," I told him.

"Thanks for helping me forget."

"Did you really forget?"

He hunched a shoulder. "For a minute."

I smiled. "Well, every minute counts."

We stood there for a moment, staring at each other. After everything we'd shared recently, I hadn't expected the awkwardness. At the same time, I couldn't bring myself to say anything.

Preston did the talking for me, though, when he said, "This isn't how I imagined this night ending."

I swallowed. "How did you imagine it?"

He tugged me to him and kissed me. "With you riding my dick," he murmured against my lips.

"In that case," I breathed. "I'd better get naked then, huh?"

His mouth met mine again and we stumbled into my house. Preston kicked my door closed while I struggled to remove my clothes, then his. He picked me up and carried me over to the couch and fell back against the cushions. "Feel free to take your time," he instructed. "I can do this all night."

I smirked. "That's good to know."

We made fast love, coming in a matter of minutes, our mouths sealed to each other. And all I could think of was...*I want more.*

Chapter Twelve

LET IT BURN

Preston

With everything I'd gone through, I tended to be the glass-half-empty type with a shot of optimism reserved only for business. Because I excelled at my job. I loved the science of building design, from planning to development to implementation. I enjoyed preparing drawings and blueprints, compiling feasibility reports, creating project proposals, and estimating costs. Work had been the one part of my life I could control, so I gave it my all. Lately, though, the focus on my career had started to wane. And it was all because of Dallas.

The past month and a half spent with her had turned my well-controlled life upside down. Not in a bad way, either. Initially, I'd thought it'd be fun to hang out with her, get to know her in a different way. I hadn't really gone into this expecting us to cross the line. Maybe I'd thought we'd have sex once or twice, but not daily. Yet, that's exactly what had happened after we'd gone to Tristan's birthday celebration a couple of weeks ago.

I'd planned for the fundraisers, the outings, and even dinners. After all, we'd started this entire thing to help her clinch the coveted spot in the Color of Law organization. What I didn't plan for were the movie nights, the private chats, the double dates with her sister, the lazy mornings wrapped around each other. All of those things were outside of the scope of our initial agreement but were nonetheless important to me. Our business relationship had somehow morphed into mostly pleasure. And as time sped toward the induction ceremony, I wondered if everything we'd shared would fade as fast as this fake relationship had started.

The bombshell revelation that Hayes wasn't my biological father had thrown me for a loop, but it could've been much worse. I could've experienced this alone. I could've been left to pick up the pieces myself. Yet, Dallas had been right there with me—supportive, encouraging, and even sweet during one of the worst times of my life. And she was here today, with her contagious smile, chatting with my new siblings while I was glowering in the corner.

When we'd arrived in Wellspring that morning, Brooklyn had greeted me with a hug. From there, it had been a whirlwind of introductions, brunch at the hotel, a tour of the small town, and now an early dinner at Bryson's home. According to Brooklyn, Senior had left the house to Bryson in his will with the stipulation that the youngest Wells sibling live there for a year, which had been hard due to the abuse he'd suffered at our father's hands.

"Overwhelming, huh?" Veronica said as she approached me.

After meeting all of them, I found I related most to Veronica because of our late entry into the clan. She'd moved to Wellspring after Senior died, had thrived in the town, and had even fallen in love.

"Pretty much," I admitted softly. "How did you do it?"

She shrugged. "I just did. And I'm better for it." Ronnie sipped her drink. "I will say that they're some of the most genuine people I've ever met. It was easy to love them."

I actually believed her. Parker Jr., Brooklyn, and Bryson had been nothing but hospitable the entire time I was there. In these types of situations, I'd expect them to be wary of me and maybe even accusatory. It was no secret the Wells family was very wealthy. I wouldn't be surprised if other siblings came out of the woodwork claiming to be illegitimate offspring of the notorious philanderer, Parker Wells Sr. "It's an adjustment," I mumbled. "I grew up thinking I was an only child. Now, I have four siblings."

"Me too." She smiled at her boyfriend, Juke, when he handed her a plate of veggies. Once he'd left us, she said, "I always knew about Senior, but thank God, I never experienced him up close and personal."

I snickered. "I guess that is something to be thankful for." Living with my mother was no treat, but from all accounts, it would've been ten times worse if Senior had been in the picture.

Bryson joined us a few minutes later. "Are you two okay over here?"

Dallas never left my line of sight. I'd watched her rock one of the babies, laugh with Bryson's wife, Jordan, and hug another woman who'd just arrived at the house. "We're good," I said.

"You seem like the quiet type," Bryson observed. "I guess we have that in common."

"You think you're quiet?" Veronica muttered.

Bryson shoved Ronnie with his shoulder. "Shut up. Give us a minute."

"Be nice." Veronica grinned and headed toward Dallas, who was now talking to Brooklyn.

I gave Bryson a sideways glance. "Do I have something to be worried about?"

He shrugged. "Why do you ask?"

"She told you to be nice. Are you not nice?"

He waved a dismissive hand toward Veronica, who waved at him as if she knew he was about to talk about her. "Time has changed me. When Ronnie met me, I was a little quiet. But never mean." He stared ahead. "My father wasn't the type of man anyone would want to know, especially if you were his son."

"Everyone keeps telling me that."

"'Cause it's the truth. We're good because of each other."

I thought about his words and wondered if I'd ever get to the place where *I* was good because of them. My heart wanted the relationship, but years of being Kenya's son had made an indelible mark on me. "I'm not used to all this family."

Bryson lifted a brow. "And you're with Dallas? Her family is huge."

I chuckled. "It's kind of complicated."

"It doesn't look that complicated to me. She's here with you. And you haven't let her out of your sight since you've been here."

"Noticed that, huh?"

"Something tells me we're alike in that way, me and you. We observe, learn everything we need to know while everyone else is talking."

Bryson's assessment was spot on. I'd rather observe than talk any day of the week. It's one of the reasons I'd made it this long. "You would be correct."

"Yep." He clasped my shoulder. "I knew it."

Parker walked over to us. "What do you know?"

"That some Wells genes are actually helpful," Bryson said. "I have to check on the twins. They're a little too quiet. I'm sure they're tearing some shit up somewhere."

"How's it going?" Parker asked me. "Ready to run screaming yet?"

"Not at all."

"It's always hard to come into a situation like this. Veronica handled it with grace when she did it, and you have too."

Curious, I asked, "How do *you* feel about this?" Up until now, Parker Jr. had been the big brother of the group, the first-born. "I've only been here for a couple of hours, but I can see you're the leader of this family."

"Honestly, I was a bit uneasy about this meeting. But now I welcome the opportunity to get to know you. It'll be cool not to be the oldest."

"I want you to know I'm not here for money."

He frowned. "Oh, I know. Prescott-Hayes is a pretty successful company—and growing."

I smiled. "Did your research?"

"Always. But I've spoken to everyone, and we all agreed you're entitled to something."

Shaking my head, I reiterated I didn't want any money from them. "I'm not here for that. I just wanted to come here and meet you all."

Parker and I talked a little about the business and he invited me back to Wellspring for a longer visit next month. Soon, Dallas and I said our goodbyes and started the three-hour drive back to Ann Arbor.

"Thanks for convincing me to come," I told her.

She laughed. "It took a lot to get your stubborn ass in the car."

"Well, you did a pretty good job of catching me off guard." That morning, she'd awakened me with her mouth around my dick and an idea for an impromptu trip to Wellspring. Despite my initial response of no, she'd made valid points about why it was important to get the meeting done.

Dallas smirked. "I told you I have my ways." She glanced down at her phone and cursed. "This fool gets on my last nerve."

I frowned. "What's up?"

"Kimball's ass. He just texted me."

The mere mention of his name pissed me off. I wouldn't have minded wearing his ass out on that golf course. "What did he want?"

"I have no idea. He only sent a one-word text. *Hi.* I feel like I'm dealing with a toddler. WAP muthafucka."

Confused, I said, "I'm not into that new hip hop, but doesn't that mean—"

"I know what it means. In Kimball's case, it's not what he *has*, it's what he *is*. A Whiny-Ass Pussy."

I barked out a laugh. She did too. "You're silly for that," I told her.

"I love to hear you laugh," she murmured, a smile still on her lips. "It's nice."

I held my hand out and she slid hers into mine. "I like that you make me laugh. Even when I don't want to."

"Well, I guess I have to make up more corny jokes."

I lifted her palm to my lips and kissed it. "I'm here for it." *I'm here for you.*

Today felt like the start of something new, something better. As we neared Ann Arbor, I realized I was ready for the journey. I also realized I wanted Dallas with me on the ride. Yet, while we'd steadily taken steps that brought us closer together, I wasn't sure she was ready for forever. Or even for now.

"What's your favorite song?" I eyed Dallas over the rim of my glass.

Earlier today, she'd texted me two words: *Today sucked.* And I'd immediately hopped into action, organizing a picnic on my recently purchased property on the Detroit River. After a light dinner of fried chicken, potato salad, and green beans all prepared by her mother, we'd spread out on the blankets I'd laid in the bed of my truck. My house was under construction and too dangerous for us to be inside.

Since we'd been out here, Dallas had yet to tell me why she was having a bad day. I suspected it had nothing to do with Kimball and the Color of Law stuff. It seemed to be more personal in nature. So I tried to keep the conversation to safe topics like music, until she was ready to share.

"Of all time?" she asked.

"Yeah."

"Hm..." She tapped her chin. "I love a lot of songs. Hard to narrow it down to one."

I stared at her. She was so beautiful, bathed in the sunlight. Every day, I found myself more invested in this thing between us. I didn't want it to end. "Okay, what about a song you like that people would be surprised about?"

A whisper of a smile spread over her lips. "That's easy. 'Dirty Diana.'"

"Who?" I teased.

She met my gaze. "Don't tell me you don't know about that song? It's about a woman who liked the boys in the band, a groupie. It's Michael Jackson!" She sang the first verse of the song, moving her body to the tune in her head.

When she blared the chorus in her off-key voice, I covered her mouth. Laughing, I said, "It's okay. You can stop. I don't want you to scare the fish. Or any of the neighbors."

She swatted me. "Shut it. There's no one within yelling distance."

I kissed her. "That's the way I like it." When I'd bought the house, one of the selling points was the privacy. Although the home was in an exclusive subdivision, the closest neighbor was a distance away, which suited me just fine. The breathtaking view of the river and the boathouse had sealed the deal. The previous owner had done substantial renovations, but I wanted to make the house my own. Construction had started before Memorial Day, and I expected to be able to move in after Labor Day.

"This is so nice," she said, turning to her side so she could face me.

I ran my finger down her cheek. "What's nice?"

"Being out here, away from everything. I didn't know you had this place. It's pretty amazing. I can't wait to see the finished house."

"I'm actually looking forward to moving back to the city. It's been a long time." I'd lived outside of Detroit for years, but I'd always wanted to return eventually. The resurgence of the downtown area had been great for the economy. Land was selling at top dollar, and new developments were sprouting up everywhere. It was a blessing that Prescott-Hayes had been in the mix on some of those projects. "I'm already pricing boats."

Her eyes lit up. "Oh, that's even better. I love being on the water."

I stared at her. There was nothing about Dallas that didn't intrigue me. "You continue to surprise me."

"That's what I live for." She placed a quick kiss on my nose.

"You love the outdoors, and you don't mind getting dirty. And you love the water too?"

"My parents live on a lake. And we lived in Cali for a while. I loved the beach and I enjoy boating. I remember when we were young, my parents would take us up north, and we'd spend the entire time on the water, jet skiing, swimming… Those were good times."

"Lake Michigan?"

She nodded. "Yep. Back then, they rented vacation homes. Now, they own one. We try to visit as a family at least once a year."

"That's cool. I like that your family gets together the way they do."

She smiled softly. "You'll have the same thing with your siblings."

"You're confident about that." I entwined my fingers with hers. "I'm not that sure it'll work out like that."

"I'm confident in *you*. You've already made the first move."

That visit to Wellspring had been an important step. Since then, I'd finalized my second trip. I would spend a week there in October. "Sometimes I can't help but wonder how my life would've been different had I known the truth. I missed so much time with them."

Her eyes glistened as if she was thinking about something sad. "That's hard. But you have time now. You should make the most of it."

"What was your favorite part about having siblings?"

A tear fell from her eyes, and I wiped it. "Just having someone to talk to, to love on. It wasn't always like that, though. I had my phases where I didn't want to be bothered. Duke and Dex got on my nerves right around the time we turned ten. They always had each other, building forts and shit. I wanted to go in the fort, and they wouldn't let me."

"What? How could they not let you in the fort?"

"Stop making fun of me. My feelings were so hurt about that. But anyway, we fought often, but the love was always there."

I rested my forehead against hers. "I want that," I admitted—to her and to myself.

"And you'll have that."

I brushed my lips over her forehead. It seemed as though I was in a constant state of desire for her. No matter where we were, I wanted her wrapped around me. But it wasn't just physical either. My emotional attachment to her grew stronger every day I spent with her. After this charade was over, I knew I wouldn't be okay if things went back to the way they'd been before. "You're so beautiful," I whispered.

Dallas buried her face in the blanket and grumbled. "Stop saying that." She peered up at me. "You know you don't have to ply me with compliments. I'll give you some anyway."

I pulled her into my arms. "I only say what I mean."

She pressed a soft kiss to my lips. "I like that about you. I'm the same way."

"I know."

"Can we stay like this for a while?" She snuggled into me.

"As long as you want."

She wrapped her arms around me. "It's the anniversary of his death," she confessed softly.

Only, I didn't know who *he* was. "Oh."

"Ezekiel Reid."

The name was familiar. "The basketball player?"

She nodded. "We were so close, so in love for so long. But most of our relationship happened in secret. Our families were super close and only a handful of people knew about us. We wanted to keep it to ourselves. Well, *I* wanted to keep it quiet."

"Why?"

"My reasons seem so convoluted now, but part of me always felt like it wouldn't last. I loved him, but we wanted different things in life. He loved being a pro-basketball star and I liked my lowkey life. I'd decided to open my own practice and wanted to give it my all. I couldn't do that flying out every weekend to watch his games. So it was easier to not tell anyone. If our families didn't know, there would be no expectations for weddings and babies and happily ever after."

"That must've been hard." Hearing that Dallas had loved once before didn't have the effect I thought it would have. I was just happy she felt safe enough to talk about him with me.

"The secret wasn't hard to keep. Actually, it was a thrill. He was my first kiss, the first man I ever…" She sighed. "But we were young. And *he* was younger than me. He was ready for us to go public, and I wasn't. I broke up with him on the night he died." I held her tighter, sensing she needed the support. "It's been over five years, but I can't help but think about that night. He was upset when he left me and I always wondered if that caused the accident."

"From what I read at the time, it wasn't his fault. He hit a slick spot on the expressway."

"I know, but still… I lied and told him I wasn't in love with him anymore. I saw how emotional he was when he walked out of the hotel room, and I didn't tell him to stay. I was so focused on what I wanted, even though it gutted me."

"You can't blame yourself for doing what you thought was best for you at the time. And if he knew you, if he *loved* you, he knew that."

Her chin trembled. "I've always been like this. All about business, all about my career. Sometimes I wonder what would've happened if I'd followed my heart and not my ambition."

The emotion in her eyes did something to me. It almost felt like I was looking in a mirror, listening to someone articulate my own thoughts. Relationships had never been a priority for me. I'd been with women, but I'd always kept them at a distance. No one had been more important than my work, than my goals. Now I was faced with the possibility that the woman I wanted would never make room for me. "I understand that more than you know."

"You do, don't you?"

I swallowed past the hard lump in my throat. "Absolutely."

We stayed in my truck for quite some time, until Dallas had a craving for ice cream. On the way home, I stopped off at the Cold Stone Creamery inside the Greektown Casino and bought her favorite concoction.

I wrapped my arm around Dallas. "Who eats peanut butter cookie dough ice cream?"

"You—" she held her spoon up to my mouth, "—once you try this. You'll thank me later."

I sampled the cold treat and was pleasantly surprised. I groaned. "That is good."

"Told you," she chirped. "Should've got you one."

"I'll just eat yours."

Dallas cracked up. "That's what you think."

A scream drew my attention to a crowd gathering around a lady who'd apparently passed out on the ground in front of the casino.

"I hope that woman is okay," Dallas said. "Maybe we should call someone."

"Maybe," I murmured, pulling out my phone to make that call. But as we neared the group, my heart sank. Because the woman was my mother.

"Shit," I grumbled, taking off toward my mom. "Call 911."

Chapter Thirteen

I DON'T WANNA

Preston

The DMC Detroit Receiving Hospital was crowded, with patients lying on beds in the hallway and a slew of people in the waiting room. Fortunately, my mother's arrival by ambulance and her precarious condition had enabled her to be moved to a private room within the emergency department.

It had been a few hours, and she'd been in and out of consciousness. I stared at her sleeping form, so small in the bed. The thought that our prior interaction could've been our last made me sick to my stomach. But that could've very well been the case. If I hadn't been there, if I hadn't acted so fast, she could've… Knowing that my mother could potentially kill herself with her addiction was one thing, but giving her CPR in front of the casino was something else entirely.

Everything had unfolded in slow motion. The crowd,

the flashes of cell phones recording the scene, Dallas talking to the dispatcher. Even in the midst of the chaos, her voice had centered me, cleared my mind enough to do what was necessary. So far, the doctors had pumped Mom's stomach and started an IV drip. The years of binge drinking had taken its toll on my mother's body. End-stage liver disease and acute pancreatitis. The diagnosis should've been a wakeup call when she'd received it a couple of months ago, unbeknownst to me. But she'd continued to drink, continued to do everything she shouldn't. And now she could die.

"Preston?" My mother's voice pulled me out of my thoughts.

I stood and walked over to the bed. "Ma."

Tears filled her eyes. "You came."

"I just happened to be there at the casino tonight." I'd told myself to stay calm when she woke up, but my anger wouldn't let me. "Good thing I was, because you could be dead if I wasn't." My voice cracked and I could feel my own tears burning my throat. But I continued, "If you're not going to care about yourself, maybe you could try to care about me. For once."

My mom closed her eyes. "I do care about you."

"Prove it. Get yourself together. Stop burying yourself in that bottle."

"He broke me," she whispered.

I frowned. "What are you talking about? Who is he? And what does *he* have to do with this?"

"Your father." She met my gaze then. "Your real father, Parker."

I stepped back. "I don't want to talk about this. I already know the truth. I had a DNA test and I've met his kids, my siblings. No thanks to you."

"You have every right to be angry with me." She tried

to grab my hand, but I moved out of her reach. "I haven't been the best mother to you."

My heart pounded in my chest. "I can't get into this with you right now."

She sobbed. "I have to say this, Preston. In case I don't make it."

"Don't say that," I ordered. "You can live if you want to."

"I'm not strong enough."

The first tear fell from my eyes. Because I knew she was right. She wasn't strong at all. She'd never been strong. "Mom."

"Listen to me. It was never your fault. It's just that every time I look at you, I see him. And I'm reminded of the man who promised me he loved me and never did. I'm reminded of the man who used me, then left without even saying goodbye. I'm reminded of the man who treated me as cold as the ground you're standing on." She sniffed.

"Here." I handed her a Kleenex.

"In spite of my behavior, you've exceeded all of my expectations. I'm so proud of you and the way you've risen above everything that life has given you, that I've given you." This time when she reached out for me, I held her hand. "I'm sorry."

I leaned down and kissed her brow. Because no matter what she'd done, I still couldn't turn my back on her. "You can show me you're sorry by getting treatment."

"I'll try. One of these days, I'll get this mother thing right."

"Hopefully before I turn fifty."

She shot me a wobbly smile. "Maybe?"

I sat there with her for a few more minutes. Once she'd fallen asleep for the night, I walked out to the lobby. I picked up the phone to call Dallas when I heard her voice.

"Preston?"

I turned around. Dallas was standing there with a cup of coffee in her hand. "You're still here?" Once we'd made it to the hospital, I'd told her to take my truck home and I'd figure out the rest later. But the fact that she'd stayed... "You didn't have to wait for me."

She stepped closer to me. "I wouldn't leave you."

I pulled her into my arms and held her. "Thank you." I kissed her head. "Thanks for staying."

"How's your mother?"

"She's resting now. I'll come back in the morning."

Dallas pulled away and grabbed my hand. "Okay. Let me take you home, then."

The drive home was quiet but peaceful. Dallas had driven my truck like it was her car and I was grateful she hadn't hit all the potholes on the Detroit streets. When we made it to my house, she started the shower.

Stepping in front of me, she unbuttoned my shirt and removed it. Next, she unzipped my jeans and pushed them and my underwear down. She kissed my chest, over my heart. "Let me take care of you tonight," she whispered.

I tugged her shirt up and off. "Only if you join me."

The corner of her mouth quirked up. "That can be arranged. Give me a second, okay?"

I stepped into the shower and waited. I heard the shower door open a moment later. Then, I felt her behind me. She smoothed her hand over my back before she kissed my spine. She washed me then, pampering me with her skilled hands and her kisses. She took her time on my back, my ass, and my legs, and worked her way around to my chest, my stomach, and my dick.

When her hand wrapped around my growing erection, I kissed her, holding her to me as if she were the key to my survival. And in that moment, she was. I needed her like

I'd never needed anyone or anything else. Her mouth, her body, her mind, her heart… Just her. I was lost in a haze of desire for her. *Only for her*.

Nothing was like it had been. Nothing would ever be the same for me. Now that I'd had her, I would always want her. I pinned her against the tile. "Dallas," I murmured against her skin.

"Preston," she breathed.

"I need this," I confessed under the spray of the water. "I need you." I kissed her chin, nipping her skin before kissing her again and sucking her bottom lip into my mouth. Dallas' soft pleas made me yearn to give her everything, to give her all of me. Forever. I pressed my dick against her. "Is this how you want it?"

Her beautiful brown eyes popped open. "No. Not here."

Without another word, she turned the water off and led me out of the shower into my bedroom. My body was burning with desire by the time she was finished drying me off. I reached for her to pull her closer, but she pushed me onto the mattress and climbed on top of me.

She caressed my face and brushed her mouth over mine, just as she lowered herself onto my dick. I thrust into her hard, loving the way we fit together, the way we moved together. It had always felt right, like this was the way it was supposed to be between us. Never mind the ruse, the deal, the circumstances. There was only this, only us.

Dallas gripped my short hair with her hands as she rode me, setting a pace of intense, but slow, movements that made me crazy with need. Every kiss, every touch stole something from me I knew I'd never get back. But I couldn't stop if I wanted to. *I never want to.*

It didn't take long for her to come, whispering my name as she trembled against me. And I was right behind her, letting out a low, long growl as I followed her over. I held her for a few moments, not wanting to let go of this moment—or of her.

Eventually, she lifted her head, her eyes glazed over and her lips swollen from my kisses. She smirked. "Maybe your nickname should be Damn, Preston?"

I laughed and fell back on the bed. "I think I like that."

She ran her fingers through my hair and nipped my chin. "I do too."

I rolled her over and peered down at her. "Be very careful, Dallas. I might not want to let you go." Too late. *I'm in love with her.*

Dallas searched my eyes. "Well, good thing you don't have to tonight?" She brushed her mouth over mine.

Soon, we were making love again. But in the back of my mind, her words replayed in my head. I didn't have to let go tonight, but would I have to tomorrow? Or some other time in the near future? Dallas might've meant the words as a joke, but they'd cemented that there was indeed a time limit to this arrangement. And when it was over, when she walked away… *She would destroy me.*

Dallas

"Got a minute?"

I glanced up from my laptop and smiled. "What brings you this way?"

Tristan walked into my office. "Just thought I'd come by and make your day." He set a manila envelope on my desk. "Some good reading."

I picked up the envelope. "What is it?"

He took a seat across from me. "Open it."

I did as I was told and pulled the contents out. The photographs were unmistakable. Pictures of Kimball embracing a random woman who wasn't Yasmin, snapped in some sort of beach resort. They'd been captured kissing behind a palm tree, draped over each other on a small yacht.

"Can you say busted?" I murmured.

"Exactly. I sent the pics to Skye, and she's handling it. I expect a live stream from Keshia T by tomorrow evening."

I smiled. "This is great, Tristan. Thank you."

"Hopefully, the paps will leave you alone."

I stuffed the pics back into the envelope. "Actually, I think they were already losing interest in me. Especially since I've been hanging out with Preston. He's not a celebrity, so I don't think they care much anymore. This will help, though."

"Definitely." He leaned back in his seat. "I also wanted to tell you I'm leaving town."

"Didn't you just get back?" Tristan had been missing in action since his birthday. My mother had been beside herself with worry.

He let out a heavy sigh. "I was still in town. One of my friends took those pictures for a small fee."

"Aside from the fact that we're supposed to leave for our family trip tomorrow, I really wish you'd consider staying, Tristan. It would definitely help repair some relationships." Duke hadn't mentioned the fight since that night, but I knew he was still bothered by it, because he hadn't even asked about Tristan when he'd called. "I don't like this distance between us."

"Not all siblings have good relationships. You know

that. Look at Mom and Dad. They intentionally keep their families at arm's length."

"Because there's a lot of bad blood."

He shrugged. "Same here."

"For no reason," I argued. "At some point, a talk needs to take place if there's going to be healing."

Tristan stood and walked to the window. Staring out at the street, he said, "Some things will never be the same again."

His words struck a chord with me, because I felt that way about my relationship with Preston. Somewhere along the line, my *fake* boyfriend had turned into my *real* man. Or at least the man I wanted to be with night and day. *One night, One fuck* had become too many nights and counting. And I didn't want it to stop.

"I want everything to be different, Dallas," Tristan continued, oblivious to my inner turmoil. "I enjoyed being around for the summer, playing softball and hanging out with the family. But if not being here makes it easier on everyone, I should just go."

I walked over to him and rested my head on his shoulder. "Things are not better with you gone. You can't believe that."

"You sure about that?" He lifted a questioning brow. "You don't call me Fun Killer for no reason."

I shrugged. "Everyone has a nickname."

"True, D.D." He wrapped his arm around me. "I love you."

Tristan wasn't the type to say those words. I could count on one hand the number of times he'd said it to me. Hearing it today made my heart swell. "Love you too." I hooked my arm in his. "Please reconsider. Mom and Dad will be devastated if you're not on that plane."

He peered up at the ceiling. "I don't think it's a good idea."

"Is it Demi?"

He shot me a sidelong glance. "Partly," he admitted. "I don't want to cause her any more pain."

The two of them had skirted around each other for over a decade, and it was high time they aired everything out. "Did you ever stop to think your leaving has caused her pain? You can't just tell someone how you feel and bust up."

"You're right. I should've never said anything."

"That's not the answer either."

He narrowed his eyes on me. "Does this mean you've told Preston how you really feel about him?"

I blinked. Backing away, I said, "I don't know what you're talking about. Preston and I have an understanding." And I understood I'd fucked that up royally the moment I'd fucked him again. And again. And again.

"That's good, sis. But it's also bullshit. I've seen you two together. I've seen the way he looks at you and how you look at him. If my instincts are correct, I would say he's not just your fake boyfriend."

"Too bad I don't listen to you."

He laughed and pointed at me. "Ah, you got me."

I closed my laptop and put the envelope in my bag. "I wish I could stay and kick it with you longer, but I have a lunch date."

"Conveniently."

Giggling, I said, "Seriously, I'm meeting Maya."

Tristan grinned. "Give her my love." He headed to the door. "And I'll talk to you soon."

"Tomorrow," I commanded. "I need to see you on that plane, Tristan."

"I'll think about it."

"Think hard," I shouted as he walked out.

A little later, I joined Maya at her favorite restaurant. "Hello." I kissed her on her cheek. "You always beat me."

"My morning meeting ended early." She waved the waitress over, and I placed my drink order. Once the server left, she leaned forward. "I have good news."

I smiled. "Today must be the day for that."

"How so?" she asked.

I showed Maya the pictures Tristan had brought me. "I'm thinking my stint as fodder for the gossip mags might be over soon."

She scowled as she studied the images. "He's such a dirtbag. But good riddance."

"Yeah. He's definitely not my best moment."

Maya peered at me. "I'd say you hit the lottery with Preston."

"You know the deal on that."

"I also know what I've seen."

The waitress brought my drink over. I took a sip. "It was an act," I lied. "Your idea, remember?"

"Oh, I do. But I've been around you two for a while now. I don't think you should disregard the chemistry you obviously have with him."

My mentor was observant. She'd seen what Preston and I couldn't hide even though we'd tried. And since it was futile to argue that point, I changed the subject. "So what's the good news?"

"Don't think we won't circle back around to this," she warned. "But the board has made their decision. They love you and they think you'll be an asset to the organization as a full member. They're willing to throw their support behind you in a future campaign for prosecuting attorney."

"Wow." I thought I would feel happier than I did in

that moment, because I'd worked for this. "That's great." I tried to sound excited, but I failed spectacularly.

"Dallas? Sweetie, what's going on?"

"Nothing," I lied. "I'm ecstatic."

"But...?"

In the last hour and a half, I'd received good news from my brother and my mentor. And all I could think about was Preston. I'd been essentially vindicated with that Kimball scandal and accepted by Color of Law, but the victory felt hollow. Yet, I couldn't tell Maya that. *Could I?* "Nothing," I repeated, forcing a smile. "I'm so thankful to you for your counsel, your friendship. This is a huge honor. I won't let you down." I meant that with everything in me, and I would jump in with both feet to succeed.

Maya tilted her head, studying me with wise eyes. "I've known you since you were a little girl. I can tell when something's wrong, no matter how hard you try to hide it."

I scratched the back of my neck. "Just a lot going on."

"Well, now you have two less things on your plate. You can go back to normal." She eyed me over the rim of her glass. "That's what you wanted, right?"

"Right." *What if that's not what I want*?

Everything seemed to be happening too fast. Last week, I'd spilled my guts to Preston in the bed of his truck, and now I was evaluating my future with him. Or without him. The only thing I knew for sure was it wouldn't be easy to go back to being sorta friends with him. Despite what I'd told myself, he'd become more than the ruse, more than my fake boyfriend. The perception of our relationship had become my reality. And I didn't know what the hell to do about it.

Chapter Fourteen

LEAVE THE DOOR OPEN

Preston

"Hey, Preston."

Dallas was a sight for sore eyes after the day I'd had yesterday. We hadn't seen each other since yesterday morning because I'd been busy handling my mother's care. "Hey." I pressed a kiss to her neck, her chin, and finally her lips. "Are you ready for your flight?"

"Yeah." She followed me into the kitchen. "Are you cooking breakfast? I have to be at the airport soon."

I pulled out a bowl. "If you call pouring a bowl of cereal cooking, then I guess I am."

She smiled, but it didn't reach her eyes. "While you're at it, you can pour me one of those too."

I'd discovered Dallas' love for Honeycomb cereal the first time she'd spent the night here. When I'd tried to get up and make her breakfast, she'd agreed until she'd seen my full box of cereal. After I fixed her cereal, I set the bowl in front of her, smiling when she popped one of the pieces into her mouth.

"How's your mom?" she asked. Dallas' cousin, Courtney, had facilitated the move to an inpatient rehab facility in Northern Michigan and had referred my mom to one of the best therapists in the field.

"The transfer went well with a few minor setbacks," I explained. The long drive had made my mother car sick, and the driver had been forced to pull over a couple of times. "She's all settled in her room. I can't thank you enough for asking your cousin to help."

"It's no trouble. I hope she works the program."

"I hope she does too." I wasn't fooling myself into believing all would be well after the talk I'd had with her. But I didn't feel the despair I'd felt even a few weeks ago. "The only thing I can do is give her the resources. It's up to her whether she'll use them."

"Right." She released a slow breath. "I'll say a prayer for her—and for you."

We ate our cereal in silence. I took a moment to study her, the way she stirred her spoon in her bowl over and over, her downturned mouth. Dallas wasn't usually this quiet. Normally, she'd be telling me about work, about one of her crazy clients while we ate. But today…she wasn't herself, and it concerned me. "Are you okay?" I asked.

She jumped and looked at me. "Huh?"

"You seem preoccupied. Did something happen at work yesterday?"

"No."

"Is it your family?"

She shook her head. "Not really. Tristan came by the office, though."

"He's back?"

"Apparently, he never left. He was just laying low."

I waited for her to continue. When another moment passed, I set my spoon down. "Dallas, what's wrong?"

She flattened a hand over her stomach and stood. "I got good news yesterday." She averted her gaze. "Tristan found out Kimball has been cheating on his wife. Not with me, of course. But he has pictures that'll be leaked today and, hopefully, close the door on me being the foil in their relationship."

The sinking feeling in my gut was back. But I didn't have to be a psychic to know what was coming next. I followed her to the sofa and sat next to her. "That is good news."

"But that's not it." She swallowed. It also wasn't like Dallas to beat around the bush. She was direct, which told me she was conflicted about something. "Maya told me the board is ready to move forward with my nomination to the org."

This is over. The reason Dallas seemed weird was because we'd come to the end of the charade, and she didn't know how to tell me. But I still needed to hear her say the words. Because after everything, after the nights together, the secrets shared, I wanted to hear from her own mouth that it didn't mean anything to her. "Which means...?"

"It worked."

"As in I don't have to pretend to be your fake boyfriend anymore?"

"That's what we agreed to, right?"

Everything in me wanted to challenge her on this, but I'd made the decision a long time ago to trust my instincts with her. Since I knew her to be truthful and she wasn't saying otherwise, I would take her at her word. And since she wasn't saying otherwise… "Then I guess that's it."

Dallas dropped her head, sucked in a deep breath, then glanced at me again. "I really appreciate you going out of your way to help me."

"Anytime. That's what friends do. And, if nothing else, we're friends."

"Real friends," she said. "Not sorta friends."

I heard the catch in her voice, the hesitancy on her part, but I couldn't reconcile that with her actions. She'd essentially disregarded everything we'd been to each other when she'd mentioned the agreement—as if that was *all* this was. I forced a smile. "Right."

She glanced at her watch. "Shit. I need to go, or I'll miss the flight." Picking up her purse, she walked to the door. I beat her there and opened it for her. She brushed her fingers over mine and gave me a kiss on my cheek. "I'll call you when I get back—to check on you and your mother."

"Okay," I whispered.

Dallas sucked in a shaky breath and rested her forehead against my chest. "Okay," she breathed. "Preston, I… Never mind. I have to go. Take care." Then, she ran to her car and drove away.

And just like I thought, she'd taken my heart with her.

Dallas

"HEY, SISSY." Bliss settled in next to me on the plane. "Raven stole Naija so I could get some sleep during the flight. She's teething or something."

I stared straight ahead. I knew if I talked to Bliss, I would fall apart, and I didn't have time for that.

"Sissy?" She elbowed me softly. "Are you okay?"

"I'm fine," I whispered. "Just tired."

"When did you start lying?"

I finally looked at my sister, and then the first tear fell. "Don't."

Bliss searched my eyes. "I heard Color of Law selected you to be a full member. That's great."

I averted my gaze and looked out the window. "Yeah, really great," I deadpanned. "I'm so happy."

"Isn't that what you wanted—the leadership role, status, voting power to determine what goes on within the organization?"

"I guess..."

Bliss wrapped her arms around me and squeezed. "Chair hugs...sometimes they're the best."

My sister had been through so much. She'd left an abusive relationship, had given birth, and still remained positive. Her resilience was amazing to me, but I didn't want to talk. "Thanks," I murmured.

"You didn't ask for my advice, but I'm going to give it anyway."

"Can I stop you?" I asked.

"Unfortunately, no." She patted my knee. "Sometimes we fuck up." Bliss was like Paityn in that she rarely cursed, only when she was pissed off. And even then, it didn't sound right coming from her mouth. "But once we realize it, we have an opportunity to fix it."

"What if it's too late?"

"It's not too late." She smiled. "Not if you tell him how you feel."

"How did you know?"

"You aren't as slick as you think you are. I knew that was going to happen when I agreed with the whole fake-out scheme. It's why I was so happy. I'm not The Bae Maker for no reason. I'm actually good at my job." She burrowed into her seat. "You and Preston are the perfect match. And on that note, I need to close my eyes."

I spent the entire flight thinking about Preston. Every layover, every bathroom break, every meal had been filled with thoughts of him and how he made me feel. Treasured. Respected. *Loved?* I didn't know if it was love, but it felt damn close to it. Which made it worse, because *he* should've been sitting next to me. He should've been my plus one on this trip.

By the time we made it to the yacht, I still couldn't get him off my mind. Even when Tristan showed up with a smile on his face. Even when Uncle Jax, his family, and the entire Reid family had surprised us. Nothing mattered because I couldn't stop replaying my last conversation with Preston in my head. My mind kept flashing to the haunted look in his eyes when I'd told him the *good* news.

I fucked up. And I only had myself to blame. I was too much of a coward to admit that I'd fallen hard for him.

My family noticed right away that something was wrong. Not because I had the *sad* face, but because I had the *stank* face. They gave me all the space I needed because of it. I wasn't in the mood for food, for the sea breeze, or for family time. I spent the first two days phoning it in, only showing up for dinner and one of the excursions. Other than that, I stayed to myself. Until my father pulled me aside after breakfast one morning.

Dad motioned to a lounger on the middle deck. "Have a seat, baby girl."

I plopped down and stared up at the blue sky. I didn't bother taking off my sunglasses. "What's up, Dad?"

"This isn't going to work, baby girl. I need you to talk to me. You've been sulking since we got here, and frankly, I'm concerned."

"I'm okay."

"You're not."

Once again, tears threatened to fall. "How did you and Mom make it for forty years?"

He smiled. "God first. Then, trust, forgiveness, compassion, and friendship. We realized early on that our marriage wouldn't survive if we didn't communicate. We made time for one another, setting aside at least an hour each day to talk about anything. No holds barred."

"Maybe it's just not in me to have something lasting like that."

"You're right. It's not in you."

I pulled my glasses off then. "What?"

"It's not *in* you, it's work. It's pushing yourself aside to see him. Your mother and I have been intentional with each other. She's my priority. I had to realize my job wasn't guaranteed, my kids would grow up and move out, my health might fade. But your mother would still be here with me. So, I don't walk in the house without greeting the one person who will support me forever. I don't leave without kissing the woman who has given me so much. I make sure we spend time alone, still conversing about our day, still taking walks, still traveling to new places."

As my father talked, I could imagine doing all those things with Preston—the traveling, the walks, the alone time, the kisses. "That's beautiful," I whispered.

"And possible for you. But you have to step up to bat to have a crack at hitting it out of the park."

I smiled. "I think you're taking this softball thing too far, Dad."

He laughed. "Hey, sports are a metaphor for life. I've been telling you that since you could walk." My father had wrapped life lessons in every sport. Even fencing. Sometimes things happened with no explanation and no matter how much you planned, your approach may backfire. "Like I told you before, life is about balance, Dallas. Despite your accomplishments, you haven't learned that yet."

"I thought I was getting better."

He lifted a brow. "If you were doing better, you would've asked Preston out because you *liked* him, not because you wanted to run for office."

Ouch.

"Everything is always business for you," he continued. "Life is about so much more than that. Your mother and I want all of you to experience the type of love we have for each other."

"It felt different to me," I admitted. "Being with him. I loved it."

"You loved *it*? Or you love *him*?"

"I probably love him."

He chuckled. "You're so stubborn. I don't know where you got that from."

"I like to think I'm a happy medium between you and Mom."

"Whatever you say."

I blew out a slow breath. "Okay, I do love him."

"So why aren't you with him now? Why isn't he here with us?"

I shrugged. "Because…I don't know. It's over."

"Obviously it's not if you're on this expensive yacht and walking around here like a zombie."

"I feel free when I'm with him," I explained. "It started one way and ended with me not even caring that I was selected to be in the organization. From the moment I found out, the only thing I could think about was him and how this would change things between us."

"It doesn't have to," Dad said.

"What if it does?"

"You'll never know." He sighed. "I know about you and Zeke."

My eyes flashed to his. "What? Why didn't you say anything?"

"I wanted you to come to me. But when you didn't, I figured you'd found someone else to confide in."

"Not really."

"I hate to think you've been hiding from meaningful relationships because of guilt, because you think you don't deserve to be loved. Zeke was one of my favorite people, but his death was an unfortunate accident. There was nothing you could've done to change that."

Tears flowed freely now, and I wiped them away with my sleeve. "I broke his heart."

"But you weren't driving the car."

"I just hate the thought of him thinking I didn't love him before he died."

"He knew." My father scooted his chair close to mine and hugged me. "Does Preston know?"

I looked up at him and shook my head. "I'm sure you've probably already guessed I didn't tell him."

Dad rubbed my hair, much like the way he'd done when I was a kid. "Sometimes it helps to voice our short-comings out loud. At any rate, I think it's time to remedy that." He cupped my cheek in his palm. "You're my little fixer. You've always been steady, strong. You come in the room and people breathe a sigh of relief because they know you have it all under control. So how about you fix your own life?"

My father was right. I'd spent too much time hiding from my own feelings. If one of my siblings had acted the way I did, I would've told them to get their shit together. So, it was way past time for me to take my own advice. Now, I knew what I had to do.

Chapter Fifteen

U 2 LUV

Preston

"I don't understand why you didn't just tell her how you felt." Cooper leaned back in his chair. "That's some coward-ass shit right there."

I glared at my best friend. "Says the man who literally just got his head out of his ass long enough to get Angel back."

Coop shrugged. "That's why I can say this."

Shaking my head, I finished the email I'd been typing when Coop had shown up. "I'm good on the advice. Besides, we don't do this."

"That's because you're stubborn as hell. And you still haven't told me why you didn't tell her how you felt."

The answer to that question was simple. I didn't say anything because I didn't think she wanted it. "She was ready for this to end, and she brought it back to the agreement. If she wanted more, she would've said something."

I'd told myself that every day since she left, and it still didn't make me feel better. While I'd known the arrangement was temporary, I thought I'd have a little more time to spend with her, to convince her to take a chance on us. "Since she didn't, I had to let her go."

"Man, don't settle for that shit. I know Dallas, and she's just as fucked up as you are. Hell, we're the fucked-up bunch. Except now, I have Angel and Mehki to cushion those fuck-ups. And you need Dallas to help you be less of a—"

"Say fuck-up one more time."

Cooper barked out a laugh. "Fuck-up."

We both laughed. "You're a dumb ass for that."

"And you're actually smiling. When was the last time that happened?"

I thought about his words. Coop wasn't lying. For a long time, I hadn't had much to smile about. "It's been a while."

"I'm glad she does that for you."

"She *did* that for me," I corrected.

Coop grumbled a curse. "I'm going to let you have this one. I'll talk to her when I see her."

"What exactly do you think that's going to change?"

"Don't worry about what I think. Just update me on the project so I can get out of here. Angel and Mehki are waiting back at my place." Coop had decided to keep his condo because he knew he'd be in Detroit for business often. They'd stopped off in Detroit on their way to Mackinac Island for a short getaway.

I gave Coop a quick rundown of the project timeline. "The staff is moving ahead of schedule. I feel confident that, barring any unforeseen circumstances, we'll meet the first deadline."

Coop studied the blueprints. "Good." He pointed at a

spot on the paper. "What about this land next to the lot? Is that available?"

I peered at the drawing. "It is. What are you thinking?"

"Let's find out if we can purchase it. I'd like to build a park for the kids in the area, a safe place where they can play."

The thought had crossed my mind too. Growing up, I'd wished I'd had a park I could go to and escape my house. "I'm already ahead of you on this. I've been in touch with Parks & Rec. We would need them to assume responsibility for it after the development is complete."

Coop held out his fist, and I bumped it with mine. "Bet. Let's make it happen." He picked up his phone and typed something. "Mehki is hungry. Before I go, how's your mother?"

The last week had been a difficult adjustment for Mom. She'd threatened to check herself out of the rehab center at least ten times. But things had calmed down a little. "I'm just hoping she can stay and work the program. If she doesn't, I don't know how long she'll be here." The sobering thought had kept me from embracing the anger still lying just beneath the surface. Although we'd spoken often, my mother and I had a long journey ahead before we could even talk about healing our fractured relationship.

"Let me know if you need anything, bruh. You know I'm here."

"Thanks, man. I appreciate that."

A knock on the door pulled my attention away from the document I'd just opened to show Coop. I'd let the administrative assistant go home early, so I shouted, "Come in."

Dallas poked her head into the office. "Are you sure you want to see me?" She smiled when she spotted Coop.

"You're here?" She walked in and hugged him. "I didn't know you were coming?"

"This time *you* didn't answer *your* phone," Coop said. "Because I called your ass about three times. And I texted you."

Dallas scratched her neck. "I was out of service."

"*You* were out of service?" he asked. "Or your *phone* was out of service?"

She shrugged. "Both. But me mostly." She glanced at me then. "Hi."

"Hi." I couldn't take my eyes off her and didn't even bother to hide my perusal. She was stunning. Her brown skin looked kissed by the sun, and she wore flip-flops with a long dress that hung off her shoulders. My need for her hadn't waned, despite the time and distance between us. I wanted to run my fingers through her curls. Wanted to run my tongue over her body. I wanted her.

She shifted from one foot to the other. "I just got back."

"And you came here?" I asked.

Dallas nodded.

Coop stretched. "Okay, so that's my cue."

Frowning, Dallas asked, "Where are you going?"

"Up north. I'll catch you on our way home." He kissed her cheek, gave me dap, and walked out.

Once we were alone, I gestured for her to take a seat, but she said, "I'll stand." I stood up and inched toward her. I shoved my hands in my pockets to keep myself from touching her. But as soon as I was close enough, I brushed my thumb over her chin. "You're touching me," she murmured.

I smirked. "So?"

She averted her gaze. "I missed you."

Her admission made my heart clench in my chest. Despite what I'd told Coop, the week apart had done nothing to strengthen my resolve to let her go. My house was a constant reminder of what we'd shared, because she was everywhere—on my pillow, in my dreams, in the shadows. I felt her in my bones. The verdict was in… *I love her.* The feeling was so raw, so intense, I couldn't imagine another day without her.

Dallas stepped closer. "Picture this— I'm on the Mediterranean, on a luxury yacht, with a staff at my disposal and everyone I love right there. I got everything I wanted before I left. Kimball was exposed for the trash he is, and Color of Law accepted me into the fold. I was supposed to be living my best life. But it wasn't really my best life, because you weren't there."

I traced her bottom lip with my thumb. "What are we going to do about it?"

She grinned. "Well, I came up with a plan."

Frowning, I said, "Plan?"

"Exactly. Remember when we were pretending to be in love?" I nodded, and she rushed on. "I think I could pretend a little longer."

A smile pulled at my lips. "A little?"

"A lot," she conceded.

"Let me get this straight. You want to *pretend* you love me?"

"Shit. Okay. Let's take the pretend out of this, because that does sound fucked up and I'm not really that romantic girl," she babbled. "Oh, and I definitely messed up my whole speech, which was supposed to end with us naked on your desk and not me stammering over my words. And I meant to ask you about your mom too, but I didn't. So, yeah…I'm not actually pretending to love you. I *do* love you."

There was something about Dallas being at a loss for words that endeared her to me even more, because I knew she didn't let many people see this side of her. I pulled her into a kiss, effectively stopping her babble. "You can stop talking now," I told her. "Mom is fine. And I love you too."

She wrapped her arms around me. "In that case, take my clothes off. Yours too."

I cracked up, remembering the first time she'd ever said that to me. I lifted her dress up. "I think I want you like this."

"Whatever you want. I just want you."

I kissed her again, this time pouring all of my love for her into that kiss.

"Oh, damn," she whispered, unbuckling my belt and sliding it off. She tossed it behind me. "Maybe you should take the rest of the day off?"

"As in spend the day with you?"

Her expression softened. "As in forever. Spend forever with me."

"I love you," I murmured against her lips.

"I love you too."

Dallas

Sometime later, right around Halloween

"I DON'T GIVE one loose misguided damn about how she feels. At all."

"That's harsh," Blake said. "It's not her fault Dex didn't tell her the rules."

Said *rules* were simple. Don't dress like the birthday girl. Period. "You're so soft," I grumbled. "What happened to my *fuck-her-feelings* sister? Oh, I know. She's cuddling with her boyfriend right about now."

Blake laughed. "Wrong. Because if Lennox was here, you would be on the other end of a dial tone."

"I swear, if you hang up on me for Lennox, it's on sight."

"You're always threatening me. You do realize I have a black belt. You beating my ass is kind of laughable."

"Well, I have a sword—"

"That wouldn't even be drawn before I kick you in the throat."

I chuckled. "Shut up. Now, back to the matter at hand."

"Aren't you there yet? I'm tired of this conversation. Just buy another damn costume. It's not that serious. You have other shit to think about right now. And why the hell did y'all pick a Marvel theme? I was Valkyrie last year, remember?"

"That's on Duke," I explained. "He wanted to be Deadpool."

For our birthday, we'd decided on an MCU theme. It had taken weeks to convince Preston to go as Star-Lord so I could be Gamora. He'd been adamant against "going as that chump who basically ruined everything." A few well-timed blow jobs did the trick, but my victory was short lived because Dexter's date purchased the same costume even after he'd told her it was off limits. Not a good way to endear herself to me.

"Wait," Blake said. "Deadpool? He told me he was coming as Luke Cage."

Figures. My brother's bright idea and he'd once again chosen to do the least work when it came to his costume.

"Whatever. Forget Duke. I've been trying to get Dex to give me ol' girl's number so I can call her, and he keeps telling me no."

"I don't blame him. You'll scare her away."

With a frown, I glanced at my phone. "I had to check and see if I was talking to the right sister. You're sounding suspiciously like Bliss."

"Girl, stop." Blake giggled. "Fine. Let's call the girl and cuss her ass out. Better?"

I hit the speakerphone button on my phone, turned off my car, and dug around my purse for my keys. "Shit," I murmured when my finger brushed against something wet. I pulled out my almost empty bottle of hand sanitizer. "Oh damn. My Purell spilled in my bag."

"Ugh, I hate that," Blake said. "Anyway, I'll handle Dex's boo. I'll see him this weekend at the food pantry, and I think he's bringing her. If he does, I'll make it very clear that Gamora is not who she wants to be at this party."

Recently, my brother had started dating a woman we went to college with. He seemed to genuinely like her, but none of us did. Which didn't bode well for any relationship. Even Duke didn't care for her and had voiced his disapproval loud as hell. I couldn't stand her either. And I suspected my mother had reservations about her too, but she rarely got involved in our romantic lives unless there was some sort of abuse going on.

I scanned the area in front of Preston's house. His truck was parked in the driveway, but it didn't look like he was home. I needed to talk to him sooner than later. "Thanks," I said.

"If she's not there, I don't mind telling Dex I can't stand his bougie-ass girlfriend," Blake added. "Well, I don't mind saying that even if she's standing right there."

"That's even better." I looked in my purse again.

Finally. I pulled out my keys. "So, have you thought about Secret Santa this year because I was thinking—"

"Oh, Lennox is here," she interrupted. "I promised him I would be naked and bent over the couch when he got home. Call you later. Let me know how it goes. Bye, Sissy."

Before I could respond, she'd ended the call. Laughing to myself at my sister's antics, I got out of the car and walked to the front door. It smelled like fresh-cut grass, which meant he'd once again mowed the lawn. It appeared he'd been in some sort of competition with one of his neighbors. Every time he noticed they'd cut their grass, *he* cut *his* grass; and vice versa.

Preston had moved in last month, and I'd spent a fair amount of time at his new home. I loved it here. I loved him. That love was so pure, so real, it took my breath away when I thought about him.

My father had been right about stepping up to bat and hitting the ball out of the park. Because once I'd declared my love for him, *to him*, things had changed for me. It was like those three words had unlocked something inside of me. Loving him and allowing him to love me had been the best choice. I didn't regret it.

In the short time since we'd made it official, we'd traveled, taken walks, held hands, kissed each other hello and goodbye—even in public—and just enjoyed each other. My work life had changed too. While my job was still important to me, work didn't supersede Preston and the life we were building together. Even now that I was a full member of Color of Law, I'd set hard boundaries on my time so that I could be free to do other things—sometimes with my family, other times for self-care, but mostly time with him. I'd teased Blake earlier about her and Lennox, but I'd ended a few calls prematurely myself for very good, very satisfying reasons. I didn't regret that either.

I unlocked the front door. "Preston?" I stepped into the house and tossed my purse onto a chair. After I locked the door and took off my coat, I kicked my shoes off and padded through the kitchen into the sunroom overlooking the river. "Pres—?" I gasped.

In the middle of the floor was a fort. White sheets hung from the ceiling above a bed of pillows and a thick down comforter. String lights and the glow of battery-operated candles set the mood.

"What do you think?"

I jumped at the sound of his voice behind me, whirling around to face him. "You," I breathed, suddenly speechless. The thought he'd put into this and the fact that he remembered my story about the fort made my heart skip a beat. My pulse raced as he inched toward me, a soft smile on his beautiful lips. He wore low-riding sweatpants and nothing else, and he smelled like him—like leather and fruit. *Perfect.*

"I figured it was high time you had your fort," he said.

Once he was within arm's reach, I smoothed my hands over his chest and stepped up on the tips of my toes and kissed him. "You have outdone yourself."

He trailed soft kisses up my jawline to my ear. "Oh, I'm not done yet," he murmured against my ear. "I have a whole night of treats planned, starting with a hot bath."

I beamed up at him, pushing his sweatpants down and squeezing his dick. "Only if you join me."

Turning me around, he unzipped my dress and peeled it off. "Whatever you want. This is your night."

Preston didn't make me wait for my orgasm though. He dropped to his knees and sucked my clit into his mouth right there. The feel of his tongue against me, the sound of his low hum as he tasted me made me want to cry it was so good. I braced myself as he took me higher and higher until I shattered, screaming out my release. He scooped me in his arms and carried me to the bathroom.

After my second orgasm, we finally settled into my fort —naked. With my back to his chest, we just lay there. No words, just us enjoying the moment and each other. It was the quiet times like this for me, the way he seemed to know what I was thinking, the way we communicated with our eyes and our hands and our lips. I fell a little more in love with him every time he kissed me, every time we made love. And I knew it would always be this way with him.

I lifted my head and brushed my lips over his. "This is amazing."

"It's yours." He kissed the tip of my nose. "I'm yours."

I smiled. "You're too good to me." I snuggled into him.

He entwined his fingers with mine, kissed the top of my head. "When I was a kid, I vowed that I would never let myself love someone. I didn't realize that love didn't always come with pain and regret."

Ms. Kenya had made valiant strides since her stint in rehab. She'd recently celebrated being sober for sixty days. Although Preston had been pleased with his mother's progress, I knew he'd still struggled with the resentment he felt for her and the things she'd done.

"I didn't know love could transform, set free. That's what you've done for me, baby. You gave the dead parts of me new life," he whispered. "You make me better."

Turning back to him, I wrapped my legs around his waist. "You're going to make me cry."

"Too late." He wiped a tear I didn't know had fallen off my cheek. "But it's okay. I still love you, crybaby."

I chuckled. "Stop. I'm just super emotional. It's this baby."

His eyes widened. "What?"

When I saw the first positive pregnancy test earlier, I passed out on the floor of my office. Luckily, Blake was standing there because she'd thrown a pillow down to cushion my fall before I hit the ground. After I made her buy another test, and that one came back positive too, I figured that was enough proof to actually say the words I'd been hesitant to think before I had proof. "I'm pregnant," I said. "I just found out today. I was going to tell you as soon as I walked in the door, but you distracted me with all of this—and those orgasms."

Preston chuckled, rubbing my stomach with his fingertips. "Straight up?" He met my gaze. "You're sure?"

I nodded, biting down on my lower lip. "Are you happy?" We'd talked about having kids, but it was always an in-the-future type of discussion. Not a right-now thing. Of course, we weren't thinking about that the few times we'd had sex without protection.

He cupped my face in his palms and placed the sweetest kiss to my mouth. And again, the tears spilled over my cheeks. He brushed them away with his thumbs. "I'm more than happy." He kissed both my cheeks, then my lips again. "Are you?"

Hell no was my initial reaction. But I'd slowly warmed to the idea of having a baby. And this fort? It had cemented that *he* was the only man I'd risk having stretch marks and labor pains for, even though the thought still freaked me out. "I am. I just don't want to puke. I hate throwing up."

"I'll be there every minute of this pregnancy."

I never had any doubt that he would. "I know. That's why I love you." He opened his mouth to speak, but I placed my forefinger against his lips. "Before you say anything, do not propose. We're not that corny."

He threw his head back and laughed. "I do know who I'm in love with, Dallas. I wasn't going to do that to you."

I let out a sigh of relief. "Good."

He pulled me into an embrace. "I was just going to tell you that you've made me the happiest I've ever been. I love you."

I pulled back and ran my fingers over his cheeks. I stared at him, in awe of how things had changed from a year ago. I never imagined this turn of events—from bathroom sex to a fake relationship for business' sake to everlasting love. And I couldn't wait to experience forever with him. "I love you too."

Epilogue

BUTTERFLIES

Dallas

A While Later

"We're making a mistake?" I nibbled on my bottom lip.

Preston peered up at me and lifted a questioning brow. "What?" After he finished tying my oxfords, because my belly was so damn big I couldn't see my feet or fit any of my heels, he stood. "We've already been through this."

"We're at the courthouse." Somehow, I'd convinced myself that it was okay to get married right before my scheduled caesarean delivery. The baby, *our* baby girl, was breech. Dr. Love had warned us we might have to go this route if she didn't turn in time for the due date.

"Because you said you wanted to be here," he said. "I

told you we didn't have to do this." Preston had never made me feel like we had to get married. He'd only been supportive and loving and sweet. He'd told me time and again that marriage wasn't a requirement for him, that we could love each other forever without the license and the ceremony. "Your call. What do you want to do?"

"I thought I could do it without my family, but I can't." It was *my* bright idea to elope. I knew the Judge, and she'd cleared the courtroom for the ceremony. Demi and Coop had agreed to be the witnesses. That was supposed to be it. Except… "We can't. They'll kill me. And I'd let them because I really need them here."

He smirked. "I know you do."

I let out an exaggerated sigh. "Good. So, let's go eat?"

"Shouldn't we tell the judge that we're leaving?"

I gasped. "Oh, yeah." I opened the door and yelped, smacking a hand over my mouth. Because inside the courtroom were every single last one of my family members, from my father all the way down to my niece, Naija. Even Maya was there. And so were his mother, Aunt Dot, and his siblings. Whirling around, I turned to Preston. "You!" Then, I balled.

Preston pulled me to him as I cried into his shirt. "I knew you wouldn't be able to do this without them," he explained. "So, I made it happen."

I peered up at him. "I love you so much," I breathed. "No pictures, though. I'm sure I look like a raccoon now. Hot. Mess."

He laughed softly while he dabbed my cheeks with his handkerchief. "I love you, baby. And you're perfect. Now, are you ready?"

Grinning, I nodded. "Whenever you are."

I hugged each of my guests as we walked up to the bench. Judge Reynolds performed the ceremony with lightning speed, just like I'd requested. Then, she pronounced us "Architect Extraordinaire and Marriage Broker." Everyone laughed as we sealed the deal with a kiss.

"I'm so happy," I said.

"Thank you for accepting my offer to be your fake boyfriend."

"Best decision I've ever made. Hands down."

He kissed me. "Definitely. I love you."

"Love you more."

TWO DAYS LATER, Dominique Lynn Hayes, was born. Preston had been right there the entire time, wiping my tears and whispering how much he needed me, how much he loved me. Now, as Preston rocked our baby girl in his arms, I was hit with an overwhelming amount of gratitude, of love, for him. If I hadn't taken the risk, if I hadn't let myself be open to the possibilities, I would never know the joy of being his wife and her mother.

"You did it," he whispered.

"*We* did it," I corrected.

"She's so beautiful, so perfect." He kissed my brow. "We did good."

"Damn good," I added.

He brushed his free hand over mine.

My eyes dropped to our hands. "You're touching me."

He smirked. "So? I'll be touching you forever."

God, I love this man. Grinning, I beckoned him closer with my forefinger. "I'm down with that." I kissed him. And I knew I'd only want him and the life we'd created together—our family—for the rest of our lives.

Coming Soon

He's better at the hook up or break up than you are!

So...

WHO IS PARKER WELLS SR.?

Want to know more about the Wells family?

Brooklyn, Parker Jr., Bryson, and Veronica were introduced in WELLSPRING Series—Touched By You, Enticed By You, & Pleasured By You. I followed up that series with a New Year short, ONE MORE DRINK.

Unimaginable luxury. Longstanding wealth. A powerful family empire that controls the town of Wellspring, Michigan. But three heirs are done—with all of it. Now one by one, these very different siblings are seizing control of their lives . . . and daring to find real hometown love.

TOUCHED BY YOU

She's falling hard for the troubled newcomer who saved her life —and holds dangerous secrets.

ENTICED BY YOU

When he is rear-ended by a gorgeous stranger, he finds himself torn between business and pleasure.

PLEASURED BY YOU

He's built a life for himself away from his domineering father and his hometown… but a chance meeting with the woman who has a hold on his heart changes everything.

ONE MORE DRINK

How many more drinks does she have to order before the

neighborhood bartender sees that she's not just his friend's newfound sister, but maybe *his* one chance at forever?

It's Not Me, It's You

I fake laugh every time I think about how ironic it is to be a commitment-phobe relationship therapist who is also the daughter of two world-renowned marriage and family counselors. Seriously, it's comical!

Want to know how I messed up my life? Getting arrested for stealing a priceless artifact for a tearful client.

Want to know what my biggest problem is? Spending my life teaching women how to break relationships when all I want to do is make a relationship—with him.

Want to know what that makes me? The Break-Up Expert who is questioning everything I thought I knew.

Excerpt: It's Not Me, It's You

YOUNG IN LOVE, BOOK ONE

"Well?" A soft smack to my ass followed the question, pulling me from a peaceful slumber.

I couldn't open my eyes, though. I couldn't even stretch like I normally did when I woke from a much-needed nap. If I did either or both of those things, I'd give myself away. Because there was a man behind me, a penis inside me. And I'd actually fallen asleep—during sex. *There's a first for everything.*

Things had seemed promising tonight. Tasty food, sensual music, stimulating conversation. Dr. Donell Pointer had hit all my superficial checkmarks for consent. *Looks.* Sincere brown eyes, pretty white teeth, strong body. *Voice.* He sounded like hot sex on a smooth, dark chocolate stick. *Personality.* The good doctor had charisma. I'd laughed at his jokes and had even enjoyed a debate on why soulmates didn't exist. Of course, he'd landed on the they-do side of the fence, while I'd stayed firmly on the no-the-hell-they-don't side. I wasn't one of those women… I didn't believe in soulmates or that love-at-first-sight bullshit. The only way to fully love someone was if you *knew* them. Fight me. But even though he was a sappy son of a bitch, it was okay. Because he'd earned a check in my most important wet-panties category. *Smile.* Oh. My. God. That thing lit up the room. And the tiny creases around his full lips made my decision easy. Sex. All night, preferably. But at least two times.

Except, I couldn't get through *one* time without a smidge of drool on the pillow, and not because he'd knocked me out with his prowess. Dr. Donnell was definitely fine as hell. Too bad he had no fuck game. No back-breaking. No tongue-talking. No toe-curling orgasm. If brown liquor was the devil, there had to be a worse name for bad, boring, small-ass dick. Hell? Disappointment? Underwhelming? No, tragic? Yep, that's it.

"Blake?" His low voice broke my reverie.

Sighing, I opened my eyes slowly. *Damn.* Such a shame to be so hot, yet so limp. A nod and a forced smile later, I rolled over on my back and tried not to look at his *little* problem. "Where is my…?" I spotted my dress on the floor near the door. Before I could slide off the bed and race toward the bathroom, his hand wrapped around my wrist.

"Baby, where do you think you're going? I'm not done with you."

Oh, boy. I couldn't help the hard roll of my eyes. *Lord, I promise to do better and not be a hoe if you'll just get me out of here without me having to hurt this man's feelings*. He was a friend of a friend of an associate. The last thing I needed was friend-group gossip. "I have to leave. Early meeting." I offered him another smile and a light caress on his cheek.

He pulled me closer and nuzzled his nose against my neck. "How about you stay? We can have breakfast in the morning. Together."

Shit. He just said the magic, dirty word. *Together* was

not what's up. "No need. I really have to go." I slipped out of his arms. But that hand of his remained on my wrist.

"I want to see you again. Maybe you'll give me a chance to change your mind about soulmates."

Like hell. "Not likely," I grumbled. "So, about that." I scratched my head, scrambled to find the right words. Somehow, "fuck off" seemed too harsh. "We don't have to do this. If you haven't realized yet, I'm not one of those women who needs the obligatory 'let's get together soon' speech." Shrugging, I continued, "It's probably best if we just not even try."

"Blake, you're a beautiful woman."

Can he just shut the hell up?

"I had a good time with you tonight." He brushed his thumb over my nipple.

I really have to find my panties.

Donnell rubbed his nose over my cheek and placed a chaste kiss there. "I don't want this to end."

Okay, I can live without my panties.

A mix between a groan and a whimper escaped his lips as he cupped my pussy in his palm—his *small* palm.

How the hell didn't I notice this?

"You're so beautiful," he whispered against my ear. "I want you."

Fuck the panties and the bra. I gripped his hand before his finger made contact with my clit. "Okay, stop. I'm done here." I pushed him away, stood, and picked up my dress.

"Blake?"

I rolled my eyes, slipping my dress on quickly. Luckily I'd chosen the comfortable, flowy maxi dress over the sexy, short black dress I'd considered wearing. Turning to him, I met his waiting, pitiful gaze. "Dr. Pointer, thanks for tonight. But I'm not interested in more of this." I motioned toward the bed. "It was…" I stopped short of saying it was nice, because I made it a habit not to lie. "Thanks for dinner and the…conversation."

Bolting from the room, I slammed the door shut and leaned against it to catch my breath. I ran my fingers through my probably fucked-up hair and hurried out of the hotel.

Acknowledgments

#25!!! Hard to believe I've written 25 books! I feel so blessed!

God first! I want to thank Him for His protection, His provision, His grace, His love.

To my hubby, Jason, thank you for being my hero. Your quiet strength calms my storms. I love you so much.

To my lit sisters, Angie, Sherelle, and Sheryl… Thanks for ZOOM sprints, for the late calls, for encouraging me, for having my back. Love y'all!!

Lina, when you talk, I listen. I love that I have seniority in your life! (Insider. LOL)

Midnight, Shavonna, Loretta, Matysha… You are the best!!! Thank you for rolling with me.

A special shout-out to the awesome readers , bloggers, and writers that I've met on this journey. Thanks for your support. I appreciate you!

Connect with Elle!

Subscribe to my Newsletter
New Releases, Upcoming projects, and Freebies!

On Facebook,
Join my cocktail lounge for exclusive updates, drink recipes, and lots of fun!
bit.ly/EllesCocktailLounge

Visit my website: www.ellewright.com

Email me at info@ellewright.com

facebook.com/ellewrightauthor
twitter.com/LWrightAuthor
instagram.com/lwrightauthor
amazon.com/Elle-Wright/e/B00VMEWB78

Also by Elle Wright

Contemporary Romance

Edge of Scandal Series

The Forbidden Man

His All Night

Her Kind of Man

All He Wants for Christmas

Once Upon a Series

Beyond Forever (Once Upon a Bridesmaid)

Beyond Ever After (Once Upon a Baby)

Finding Cooper (Once Upon a Funeral)

Jacksons of Ann Arbor

It's Always Been You

Wherever You Are

Because Of You

All For You

Wellspring Series

Touched By You

Enticed By You

Pleasured By You

Pure Talent Series

The Way You Tempt Me

The Way You Hold Me

The Way You Love Me

Distinguished Gentlemen Series

The Closing Bid

Women of Park Manor

Her Little Secret

Carnivale Chronicles

Irresistible Temptation

New Year Bae-Solutions

One More Drink

Young In Love Series

It's Not Me, It's You

Historical Romance

DECADES: A Journey of African American Romance

Made To Hold You (The 80s)

Suspense/Thriller

Basement Level 5: Never Scared

About the Author

There was never a time when Elle Wright wasn't about to start a book, wasn't already deep in a book—or had just finished one. She grew up believing in the importance of reading, and became a lover of all things romance when her mother gave her her first romance novel. She lives in Michigan.

Connect with Elle!
www.ellewright.com
info@ellewright.com

Made in the USA
Monee, IL
26 December 2023